In the Convent

A Frances Yates Mystery

by

Marjorie G. Jones

DORRANCE
PUBLISHING CO
EST. 1920
PITTSBURGH, PENNSYLVANIA 15238

Dorrance Publishing Co
585 Alpha Drive
Suite 103
Pittsburgh, PA 15238
Visit our website at *www.dorrancebookstore.com*

ISBN: 978-1-6470-2348-5
eISBN: 978-1-6470-2976-0

Exceptional book! Marjorie Jones has repeated her success as an author yet again. Marjorie is a master at bringing readers behind the closed doors of sacred places, and pulling back the curtain of mysterious spaces. *In the Convent* takes you on a fascinating exploration of history, humor, mystery, mayhem, faith, and friendship!

Travel with Dame Frances Yates to Mexico and immerse yourself in the sights, smells, and tastes of the journey! Go behind the scenes *In the Convent*, as Dame Frances Yates and her companions attempt to solve yet another crime and do so with gusto.

The book is full of surprises. Turning conventional wisdom on its head, Marjorie Jones is able to bring insight and expertise to hidden rules and righteous explanations.

Never one to avoid controversial topics, the book brings fresh perspectives to contentious topics of women's ordination, clericalism, and the challenges of religious life today.

Volatile topics like women's ordination, the plague of clericalism and the challenges of religious life are not off-limits *In the Convent*.

There is no doubt that Dame Frances Yates and her companions are the cast you want around when the going gets rough, and rules need to be broken.

I guarantee you, you will not be disappointed with *In the Convent*!

Carefully crafted and thoughtfully written, *In the Convent* is more than a book about a crime to be solved -- it's an exploration of faith, mystery, and friendship.

One never knows what to expect *In the Convent*, and be assured that the journey to a foreign land with Dame Frances Yates and her companions is worth every minute of your time reading this terrific book.

— *Michael J. Castrilli*

Dame Frances Yates, detective, historian, spiritual explorer, has landed in Mexico! Accompanied by her intelligent sidekicks, a former student and her Scotland Yard husband on their honeymoon, Frances remains very much herself (Deliciados replacing her beloved British cigarettes) as she solves a death in a convent. The murder has wide reverberations: the dedicated sisters have discovered the syncretic Great Goddess (Mary? The Corn Goddess Tonantzin?) and Her many feminist implications, triggering a backlash from a very nervous patriarchy.

— *Kathy Chamberlain, Nov. 9, 2019*

To Exemplary Students
at
Sing Sing and Graterford/Phoenix Prisons

All biography is story-telling. No life is a code to be deciphered: There will always be gaps and inconsistencies, and it is stories that make the missing connections.

—Laura Thompson,
Agatha Christie: An English Mystery

In the Gilded Cage of English civilization, I think longingly of American wilds and anything that reminds me of them is a pleasure.

—Adela Breton

Chapter One

"Good Lord, it's hot!" Dame Frances Yates gasped as she exited the plane at Mexico City.

Most unexpectedly, the renowned British historian found herself for the first time in her long life in Latin America. After a trans-Atlantic flight to New York, where she witnessed the wedding of Inspector Stuart Drummond of Scotland Yard and Elizabeth Wolcott, her former student at the Warburg Institute in London, quite impetuously, and since she'd already be halfway there, Frances had decided to accept another invitation.

When he learned about her visit to New York, another former student, Juan Carlos Ortiz, had invited Frances to fly on from New York to spend a few days in the Mexican capital. He had made arrangements for her to give a talk regarding Giordano Bruno and the Hermetic tradition in the Convent of famed seventeenth century nun Sor Juana de la Cruz. In turn, when Elizabeth and Drummond learned of Frances's travel plans, they asked if they might accompany her and spend their honeymoon in the Mexican capital.

Although Elizabeth had visited the country several times and was enthralled with everything Mexican, she relished the chance to share its cultural riches with her new husband, and of course, Frances was delighted. It would be reassuring to have companions on the long journey, and she had grown very fond of the "redirected" American lawyer, who had transformed herself into a Renaissance historian, and her handsome new husband. Since their recent collaboration involving a crime at the Warburg

Institute in London, Frances now affectionately referred to the newlyweds as her "partners in crime."

The trip was to be more or less a reunion of the seminar last year when, in the midst of exploring the history and meaning of Tarot cards, Frances also had been forced to unravel the mysterious death of a Warburg librarian. Happily, this expedition promised only adventure and celebration.

Significantly, during his sabbatical at the Warburg, Juan Carlos had introduced Frances to seventeenth century *religiosa* Sor Juana de la Cruz, the subject of his ongoing dissertation regarding the influence of the Hermetic tradition in Mexico. Now having read Octavio Paz's brilliant biography of the remarkable Mexican scholar, mystic, and feminist, Frances was especially intrigued by the opportunity to acquire at least a sense of Sor Juana's cultural context. What a revelation to learn the Hermetic tradition appeared to have found its way across the vast ocean—to a woman no less—in Colonial Mexico so soon after Bruno's martyrdom at the Campo dei Fiori in 1600!

When first she had informed her dearest friend Warburg director Frida Hilb of the extraordinary invitation, Frida ardently encouraged her to make the trip. The next day she informed her in the spirit of Aby Warburg's memorable trip to the American southwest early in the twentieth century, the Warburg would pay for her airfare from New York to Mexico City and back to London.

Before her departure, however, Frida had assigned some homework to Frances, insisting she read Sybille Bedford's enticing 1953 travel classic *A Visit to Don Otavio* and Rebecca West's *Survivor in Mexico*, which mirrored her renowned *Black Lamb, Gray Falcon* regarding her peregrinations through the Balkans. Both books in turn had led to Scottish-born Frances Erskine Inglis's remarkable *Life in Mexico*, written in 1842, when she was the wife of the first Spanish ambassador to newly independent Mexico.

"Something about Mexico has enchanted our compatriots, Frances. There is a substantial genre of women's travelogues about the place. Really I envy you!" Frida exuded. "Remember, Aby Warburg, too, was fascinated with his expedition to the American southwest and the similarities he encountered there between indigenous cultures and ancient traditions in the Middle East."

Frida further reminded Frances of the improbable and ill-fated story of Austrian Emperor Maximillian and the Empress Carlota, as depicted in the striking Manet portrayal at the National Gallery. Vaguely Frances recollected the violent scene, which she had managed to ignore each time she passed by on her way to view another exhibit at the National Gallery. Now in preparation for her trip, she intended to look at the painting more carefully and suggested she and Frida do so together followed, of course, by tea and sweets at the Gallery tearoom.

Ever the diligent student, Frances soon revisited the Manet and devoured all of the assigned reading, including another volume by an American she discovered on her own, Frances Parkinson Keyes' charming *The Grace of Guadalupe*, written in 1951. As a result, even before she stepped foot in Mexico, she was enthralled and primed for adventure!

The Execution of Emperor Maximilian by Edouard Manet

Chapter Two

As soon as she saw tall, handsome, and elegant Juan Carlos waiting for her at the foot of the plane's steep stairway, Frances forgot the oppressive heat and waving eagerly, broke into a grin. With Inspector Drummond supporting her left elbow and holding tightly on to the metal railing, she made her way gingerly down the steep, narrow steps. Smiling, Elizabeth Wolcott-Drummond, as she now called herself, followed closely behind. (Traditionalist Frances was pleased the feisty American lawyer had decided to link her own name to that of her new husband.)

"*Bienvenida en Mexico, querida Dama Francesca*!" gallant Juan Carlos greeted her with a small bouquet of colorful blossoms and warm *beso* on each cheek, the first time the two had acknowledged one another with a gesture beyond a formal, delicate half-handshake.

Yet in this time and place, the affection felt appropriate and genuine, as eagerly Juan Carlos similarly greeted Elizabeth, heartily shook hands with Inspector Drummond, and congratulated the two colleagues on their marriage.

Since it was a lengthy walk to the terminal, Juan Carlos had arranged a wheelchair for Frances, who, far from agile, accepted gratefully.

"Quite satisfactory," she observed as her three companions, two confident, handsome gentlemen and a caring, capable intelligent female companion, navigated her through quite casual and cordial customs and collected their baggage.

Once through the terminal, a spacious air-conditioned car awaited beside an attendant.

"How thoughtful, Juan Carlos," Elizabeth observed.

With Frances ensconced in the front seat, Juan Carlos behind the wheel, and Drummond and Elizabeth Wolcott-Drummond holding hands in the back seat, everyone began to talk at once.

Although the air-conditioned car was a relief from the oppressive heat, familiar with Frances's habits and foibles, Juan Carlos immediately opened the windows, and indeed, as soon as she was more or less buckled into her seat, Frances opened her purse and lit a Woodbine. Immediately the entire vehicle was enveloped in a cloud of malodorous tobacco smoke.

"Yes, the wedding was lovely," Elizabeth exclaimed. "After the ceremony in the chapel at Calvary Episcopal Church on Park Avenue, officiated by both an Episcopalian priest and my Unitarian minister, our guests strolled across bucolic Gramercy Park to the historic National Arts Club where Dame Frances gave a most charming toast, taking full credit for our marriage!"

Beaming and nodding, Frances affirmed, "Which of course is true!"

Her English colleagues had never been to Mexico and couldn't wait to see the sights Elizabeth had noted, including an ancient indigenous pyramid, the renowned murals of Diego Rivera, along with the paintings of his exotic gifted wife, Frida Kahlo.

"*Bueno*, but tonight we must celebrate a la Mexicana," Juan Carlos insisted in charmingly accented fluent English.

As he confidently weaved in and around the daunting congested traffic of the Mexican capital, Juan Carlos pointed out Chapultepec castle, which loomed over an entire mountain top and centered the metropolis.

"Mexico City, or Tenochtitlan, as it was known in ancient times, was once the largest city in the world," he informed them. Then recounting some of the tragic history of the ill-fated imperial mission of Austrian prince Maximilian and his wife Carlota in the nineteenth century, Juan Carlos suggested a visit to castle, prompting Frances to note knowledgably the Manet in the National Gallery.

Chapter Three

In the heart of the city, the car stopped before the entrance of the grand Majestic Hotel at the edge of the bustling Zócalo. Astonished by the vast plaza, Frances exclaimed it reminded her of the Campo dei Fiori in Rome, where in 1600, her hero Bruno was martyred by the Inquisition. To herself she acknowledged a sense of European cultural arrogance that had left her unprepared for European historical grandeur on the American side of the Atlantic.

"Since it is near both the Cathedral and Convent of San Jeronimo, I thought you'd be comfortable here, Dama Francesca, although I must caution that quite early in the morning you're likely to be disturbed by the blaring of trumpets as the official Mexican flags are raised in the square."

When the solicitous doorman opened the door, offered his hand to help her out of the car, and greeted her personally, "*Buenos dios, Profesora Yates, bienvenida a l'Hotel 'Mayestic*," Frances was enthralled.

"Oh my, they are expecting me and know my name...really, Juan Carlos, this is superb," she raved.

After the doorman had escorted her up the front steps into the elegant lobby, again Frances was startled. With lofty arched ceiling and tiled floor, the Majestic had an old-world grandeur with a decidedly Spanish panache.

At the desk, a gracious clerk welcomed Frances and directed her to *habitacion* #535 facing the Zócalo. While Elizabeth accompanied Frances and a charming English-speaking young bellhop to the room, Juan Carlos invited Drummond to join him for a cold Dos Equis in the Cantina, the hotel's handsome wood and mirrored bar.

High ceilinged and spacious with thick, dark green carpeting and handsome aged mahogany furniture, #535 resembled an elegant English drawing room. Reaching nearly from ceiling to floor, French windows, veiled with delicate white lace curtains waving in a gentle breeze, opened onto a narrow, ornate, wrought iron balcony overlooking the Zócalo.

Encouraged by the solicitous bellhop, Frances stepped onto the balcony and, as directed, to the left saw a magnificent seventeenth century cathedral that rivaled any in Europe. Directly across the square was the sprawling National Palace where, Juan Carlos had informed her, Diego Rivera's magnificent murals depicting the history of Mexico were enshrined.

Although terribly warm and fatigued by the long flight and time lag between New York and Mexico, Frances was delighted—even more so when Elizabeth, who had helped her unpack, informed her there would be time for a tub and nap before dinner at eight.

"In the meantime, I hope the cathedral bells and mariachi music from the Zócalo don't prevent you from snoozing, but if you need us for anything, Stuart and I are staying a floor below in room 435 and could meet you in the lobby then."

"How lovely—really everything is quite lovely!" Frances repeated as she surveyed the surroundings with satisfaction. Fresh snow-white sheets, a deep, footed porcelain tub in the colorfully tiled bathroom, and a graceful bouquet of white calla lilies in a tall, slender, azure blue pottery vase on the bureau—a gift, the attached card informed her, from Juan Carlos enveloped Frances in a blanket of pleasure and anticipation.

By the time Elizabeth let herself into their room on the floor below Frances' room in the Majestic, her new husband, showered and shaved with a fresh white shirt, dark slacks, and argyle socks (minus tie and shoes), was propped on several pillows and stretched out on the double bed. Putting aside his green Michelin guide to Mexico, he smiled and opened his arms into which Elizabeth folded blissfully. As always, and especially after a long day travelling across a continent, how good he smelled to her! After a lingering, gentle kiss, and as she settled into the welcoming crook of his strong arm, Elizabeth breathed a sigh of relief.

"Oh, my darling, what a day this has been! Did you ever imagine we'd find ourselves on a Mexican honeymoon, chaperoning an esteemed Dame of the British Empire?"

"Well, for that matter, my dear," Drummond chuckled as he held her securely, "if someone had told me the day I was called to the Warburg Institute to investigate a homicide, beyond apprehending the culprit, I would become immersed in the Hermetic tradition and fall in love with an American lawyer, I would have thought it a fairy tale. Now that I think about it, perhaps it is!"

"Me too, and lucky us!" Elizabeth laughed, kissing his smooth cheek, fragrant with the aftershave that, like a bee to honey, had first attracted her to him. Of course, his clipped British accent and subtle sense of humor heightened the charm. "But right now, since Dame Frances is safe and secure upstairs for a few hours, I too could use a shower and nap. Then Juan Carlos is taking us all out to dinner, and Wednesday, after escorting Dame Frances to the Convent for her talk, he would like to take us to the castle at Chapultepec. *O, caro mio,*" she exclaimed with another quick kiss, "*Mexico me gusta mucho!*"

Chapter Four

Meanwhile on the floor above, exhausted Frances looked forward to a tub and nap. Blissfully, she submerged into a warm bath sprinkled with lavender scented Flor Blanca sea salt she found in a tray at the side of the tub, but while retrieving a Woodbine from the dwindling supply in her purse, she fretted, "Since I'll be here for an entire week, and if there is such a thing, I wonder whether I might try a Mexican cigarette..."

Then, as she exhaled and leaned back against the curved porcelain tub in the soothing fragrant suds, Frances reflected on events in London that had led to her most improbable adventure yet.

As she did, she noticed on the wall facing the tub a colorful print of exotic flowers that resembled the lavish bouquet Juan Carlos had ordered placed in her room—by design, she surmised, to replicate the print. When she emerged awkwardly and slowly from the tub and donned the thick, freshly laundered white terry cloth robe hanging behind the door, she saw the print was by Diego Rivera. Last year, when she was writing an article about the cards, she seemed to see Tarot everywhere. Yet here in her first moments in Mexico, the precisely delineated *Flower Festival* reminded her of the cards. *Are the precise number of blossoms significant?* she wondered.

Then with the light breeze from the Zócalo cooling the room, Frances slipped between the fragrant fresh sheets, and as she drifted into a blissful nap, reflected, "There was so much more to see and learn in Mexico..."

Flower Festival: Feast of Santa Anita by Diego Rivera

Chapter Five

That evening at a charming bistro Juan Carlos had selected for their first dinner in Mexico, refreshed by baths and naps, the four colleagues dined outdoors in a vibrant garden lit with candles and lanterns strung among the trees. Seated at a large, round table covered with a striped blue-and-white cloth, they pondered the exotic bilingual menu, but what to choose was another matter for Frances, since, to say the least, she was not an adventuresome eater. Having spent several months studying and dining at the Warburg Institute, as well as London pubs, quickly Juan Carlos perceived the problem.

"Perhaps I can assist, Dama Francesca. May I suggest creamy corn soup and baked capon *sin salsa*? Although not very spicy, both are flavorful and tasty."

"Thank you, Juan Carlos," Frances nodded with relief.

On the other hand, delighted with the enticing options, Elizabeth and Drummond selected coconut-crusted tilapia and *carne asada,* both dishes most definitely *con salsa*. Satisfied with their entrees, for dessert they all shared a huge plate of warm strawberry quesadillas, which unanimously everyone agreed was the best dessert any of them had eaten anywhere in the world!

As they waited for their food to arrive, Juan Carlos suggested, "Perhaps also, Dama Francesca, you'd like to sip a margarita, a sweet and quite refreshing Mexican cocktail."

Now eager to immerse herself in local culture, Frances agreed, and when it arrived, the thick, frothy, and fruity drink served in a frosted, stemmed

13

cocktail glass rimmed with crusted salt, glided over her tongue as smoothly as any baked custard she savored.

Throughout the evening, a cadre of charming and lovely sisters, dressed identically in long lemon-yellow skirts with fresh flowers entwined in their dark, braided hair, sang and strummed beautiful Latino melodies on guitars and violins. Enchanted, Frances found herself tapping her toes and swaying to the lilting music. Exchanging glances, Drummond and Elizabeth joined other convivial patrons on the dance floor.

Seeing the effects of the margarita displayed in the glow on her smiling face and gently clapping hands, and emboldened by the ever-enticing concoction, Juan Carlos dared the unimaginable, "Dama Francesca, would you care to dance?"

"Oh, my dear Juan Carlos, I couldn't...why, I haven't danced in more than half a century!"

"But neither have you been in Mexico, where everyone knows margaritas go directly to your feet!" he responded, offering his hand.

Virtually lifting her from her seat, the handsome young Mexican and aged British scholar took to the small, square dance floor, where carefully but firmly he led her in a gentle two-step in time to the throbbing guitars.

"*Dio mio*, talk about an armful," Juan Carlos mused to himself.

In fact, it was easier to lift heavy cartons of books, which he did regularly, than it was steering hefty Dame Frances Yates around a dance floor! Yet somehow, they managed, and when the music stopped, arm in arm they returned to their table where Frances eagerly took another sip of her margarita, and tipping her glass to Juan Carlos and her colleagues, toasted, "Viva Mexico!"

Chapter Six

At seven the next morning, as the flag was being raised in the Zócalo to the usual blare of significantly discordant trumpets while uniformed troops raised the Mexican flag, Frances awoke with a jolt, sat straight up in bed, and immediately pressed her hands to her throbbing temples.

"What on earth, what's happening? Where am I?" she sat up, dazed. Although she had slept soundly, along with a significant headache, she sensed a terribly upset tummy. "Oh, dear, what's happening, and what have I done?" she moaned aloud as visions of an exotic setting with tantalizing music and, above all, deliciously sweet margaritas resurged through her jumbled recollections. Unfortunately, she couldn't remember returning to the Majestic last night. "Was I dreaming, or did I actually dance with charming Juan Carlos? Could this be what they call a hangover?" she pondered.

If so, it was not only a compound word, which she noted habitually, but the first of her long life. Since she wasn't sure how best to address it, Frances mourned her worldlier sister wasn't in Mexico to counsel and care for her, as she always did.

In her eighties and a decade older than Frances, seemingly tireless Ruby had declined to join Frances on the long trans-Atlantic flight, followed by still another to far away Mexico—to say nothing of return flights home. Claiming she didn't have the stamina, she was further reluctant to absent herself for several weeks from her responsibilities at their beloved home and Holy Trinity church in Claygate.

Perhaps instead she could seek sensible Elizabeth's advice, although, given her hazy reminiscences of her uncharacteristic participation during a most delightful and festive evening, she wasn't sure that would be prudent. Further she didn't want to intrude on the newlyweds so early in the morning. Instead, recalling she had a breakfast date with Juan Carlos at nine in the hotel dining room before their scheduled visit to the Convent, she summoned all of her English fortitude, struggled out of bed, and headed to the cool, tiled bathroom, where dizzily she shed her worn flowered cotton nighty and white socks, which—regardless of the temperature—she needed to keep her perpetually cold toes warm. Brushing her teeth helped clear her head, and thankfully, rummaging in her travel kit, she found a small bottle of aspirin and minty antacid tablets from Boot's ever-reliable Ruby had thought to include among her supplies.

Somewhat restored as always by another warm bath and a large glass of Topo Chico fizzy water from the bottle she found in the small fridge tucked next to the bureau, Frances managed to assemble her costume for the day: Her usual dark gabardine skirt with a fresh striped cotton blouse and her favorite and very worn navy blue jacket, thick stockings held at the knee with garters, and sturdy walking shoes. Feeling somewhat revived, she was surprised to find herself hungry and anticipating breakfast.

When Frances emerged from the elevator, how reassuring once again to see handsome Juan Carlos reading a newspaper in a club chair across the lobby. Wearing a navy blue blazer with a fresh, light green shirt and tie with stripes the color of the Mexican flag, he was clean shaven and bright-eyed. In light of the previous evening's celebration, he also was relieved Frances seemed alert and steady. Immediately he rose to greet her and, gently taking her arm, guided her toward an escalator for the short ride to the charming balcony restaurant overlooking the Zócalo. There Elizabeth and Drummond already were seated at a square table with a fresh, starched white cloth near the open bay windows. As soon as they saw her, both waved and rose to their feet. While Drummond held a chair for Frances, he and Elizabeth exchanged glances and breathed a sigh of relief; earlier they had wondered whether, in light of last evening's festivities, she would be able to function today, but thankfully this morning she seemed alive and well. Indeed, as soon as she spotted a lavish breakfast buffet that made her mouth water, she immediately departed to survey the feast.

"What a trooper!" Elizabeth exclaimed as Frances delved into the buffet. The variety of choices was so dazzling she didn't know how or where to launch her attack, yet just a few minutes later she returned to the table with a warm, heavy, white china plate piled high with perfectly cooked fluffy scrambled eggs delicately flavored with just a hint of fragrant basil, juicy tomato halves broiled with bits of *Anejo* cheese, several thin, crisp slivers of glazed *jamon*, and bits of potatoes browned with cumin and served with sour cream along with her first warm tortilla accompanied by a spoonful of thick guava jam, and a cup of steaming *limon* tea. Suspecting she might appreciate it, Juan Carlos informed her the tea, derived from lemongrass, was helpful for an upset stomach.

Between heaping forkfuls, Frances declared, "Thank you for your hospitality, Juan Carlos, although I'm afraid I drank a bit too much of my first margarita, which was absolutely delicious. Truly, I can't remember a more festive evening!"

"It was my great pleasure, Dama Francesca," ever-gallant Juan Carlos responded. "As always, you were stimulating company, and before you leave Mexico, we must celebrate again at several other of my favorite establishments.

"Now this morning, if you are able and willing, I thought we all might stroll across the Zócalo to the convent of San Jeronimo, which isn't far beyond. It's a lovely day, and there is always a great deal going on in the plaza. Personally, I think it is one of the great spaces anywhere in the world, as well as the most effective means to provide visitors with a sense of this wonderful city that, frankly, I adore. Then tomorrow I thought we might visit the shrine of the Virgen de Guadalupe, which better than any other monument illustrates the heart and soul of Mexico."

"Lovely, along with margaritas," she smiled coyly, while scarfing more eggs with brown beans and the salty slices of ham, served with chunks of fresh papaya, followed by a second warm tortilla smothered in sweet jam, "I am anxious to absorb as much Mexican history and culture as possible in the next few days."

"Before we embark," he added, reaching into a paper bag at his feet, "I thought you might be able to use this," he said, withdrawing a smart, straw sombrero.

Like his tie, the hat was banded with the red, white, and green of the Mexican flag and appropriately stylized to the tastes of a mature, conservative British scholar.

"The sun in Mexico is both glaring and very warm," he noted, "so before we set out across the Zócalo, I thought you should be protected. You see, it compliments my tie and own hat as well," he smiled, displaying a sporty, dark straw Panama with similarly striped band.

"How perfect and typically thoughtful, Juan Carlos! Surely it will be the only one like it at Claygate and the Warburg," Frances laughed with delight while plunking her new chapeau atop her unruly mop of short, white hair, drawing a number of stares and smiles from other guests on the *terrazja*.

Chapter Seven

When finally she had finished scarfing down her substantial breakfast and placed her large, red cotton napkin on the table, Juan Carlos offered his arm and guided Dame Frances Yates in her new sombrero onto the majestic Zócalo. Walking left from the hotel, they were accompanied by the lilting music of early morning guitar players just as blue-and-white striped tented booths were opening to sell tortillas, fresh fruits, colorful hand-woven baskets ("I must acquire one for Ruby," Frances noted.), and exotic flowers like those on the poster in her room, which Juan Carlos informed her were called "*alcatraces*" in Spanish. Along the arched sidewalks *escribiendos* set up shop to write letters for *illiterati*, something Frances had never seen in any of her European travels.

"American traveler Frances Parkinson Keyes once wrote of the Zócalo that, 'All the life in the capital flows through this plaza,'" Juan Carlos observed.

"Oh dear, still another author to explore...Well, I certainly understand why she or anyone else would say that!" a mesmerized Frances affirmed.

"Before we arrive at the convent, however, for a sense of Mexico's colonial splendor I thought first we might pay a brief visit to the Cathedral," Juan Carlos suggested. "Really there are few finer examples of the Baroque anywhere. Then tomorrow for added cultural context I would like to take you, Elizabeta, and Inspector Drummond to visit the Basilica of the Virgen de Guadalupe at Tepeyac." ·

As the two historians—one aged, rumpled English woman at the zenith of her storied career, the other an earnest, young Latino at the onset of his—strolled across the massive plaza, Juan Carlos imparted some of the unique history of the ancient capital once called Tenochtitlan.

"Still another example of a student instructing his teacher," Frances acknowledged to herself.

"To begin, perhaps it will surprise you to learn this majestic plaza where we now are walking was once a grand canal. Indeed, when Cortes and his banditos arrived in 1521, the ancient capital, then called Tenochtitlan by the Aztecs, was a maze of canals, thought by some of the Europeans to rival Venezia for its beauty. In the sixteenth century, this was the largest and most hectic city in the world, and according to Mexican author Alvaro Enrigue, was considered 'the root of the world.' However, over the centuries and in the interest of commerce and efficiency, the canals were filled in, explaining why still today—because the land beneath us still is so saturated—it is not unusual some buildings tilt."

"Fascinating," all three tourists exclaimed simultaneously.

"Perhaps before you leave," Juan Carlos continued, "we can find an English translation of Enrigue's remarkable novel *Sudden Death*, which has to do with the history of tennis, first played by medieval priests, who conjured the balls as souls being batted back and forth across the net. The story takes place in Europe and Mexico in the sixteenth century, and I am certain you would appreciate and enjoy it."

"Yes, please," Frances responded. "When I return to London, I have determined to immerse myself in Mexican history and literature, since quite obviously here too in Mexico, as Europeans circled the globe in the 1500s, the forces of their imperialism and enterprise are evident."

"Certainly, Dame Frances," Juan Carlos affirmed somewhat hesitantly, "but here, I believe, the experience was unique. You see, quite incredibly, according to their intricate calendar, the very year the Aztecs were expecting the return of their redeemer god Quetzalcoal, Cortes appeared, and so, thinking their savior had arrived, the Aztec emperor Moctezuma welcomed him into the city."

"Remarkable, Juan Carlos—like Christ, still another redeemer god! Although regrettably I wasn't familiar with this version, it appears to affirm Joseph Campbell's theory these myths are universal, and of course, as you know, I maintain Bruno's message also conforms to this worldview, which helps explain why it was so threatening to Catholic theology."

"Especially in archly Catholic Spain," Juan Carlos added. "So rather than outright conquest, which would have been virtually impossible for so few *conquistadores*, here in Mexico the Spaniards more or less absorbed indigenous cultures—or perhaps I should say, it was the other way around, which again is why I propose tomorrow we visit the shrine of the Virgen de Guadalupe whose shrine illustrates this phenomenon better than any written history lesson." Then he added softly to her privately, "It means a great deal to me, Dame Frances, to be able to share the history of my country with you."

"It is I who am grateful, Juan Carlos. Indeed, it occurs to me our roles have been reversed—now it is you who are the instructor and I the pupil, which, I hasten to add, pleases me enormously. Please tell me more about Mexico City."

"It is an honor, Dame Frances," the gracious young Mexican smiled and, bowing his head, placed his hand over his heart as they mounted the steps, and between the two looming bell towers entered the soaring archway of the majestic Cathedral of the Assumption of the Most Blessed Virgin Mary into Heaven, consecrated in 1656.

Since she had spent her entire career navigating pan-European currents, naturally Frances couldn't help but place this extraordinary colonial edifice in the context of the years of Bruno's martyrdom and the eruption of the devastating Thirty Years War, which pitted mighty empire against empire and Catholic against Protestant. Thus, she viewed the magnificent cathedral as evidence of zealous determination to establish Roman Catholicism in the New World, as dreaded English Protestantism inexorably made its way to the west of the continent.

Built atop the Aztec Templo Mayor of Tenotchlitan with stones from the ancient temple used in construction of the seat of the Roman Catholic Archdiocese of Mexico and the capital of New Spain, the cathedral housed sixteen ornate chapels, each dedicated to another saint. A magnificent white marble altar crowned with Christ pendant on a giant golden Crucifix.

"While the Church has erected and maintained this magnificent monument, unfortunately, Dama Francesca, some of the same—shall we say—conservative forces that silenced Sor Juana in the 1600s are alive and well in

Mexico today," Juan Carlos ventured as they toured the sumptuous elaborate cathedral.

"What are you saying, Juan Carlos? Are you suggesting the ongoing presence of the Inquisition here in Mexico today? Surely not!"

"At risk of influencing your visit in the convent today, Dama Francesca, I think you will find a more progressive interpretation of the faith that, to say the least, is not endorsed by the current Church hierarchy in Mexico."

"Even today in this obviously vibrant cosmopolitan capital? How is that possible? Or is it another case of *plus ca change*? Needless to say, I am eager to visit the convent and appreciate your making it possible."

When they emerged an hour or so later from the dim interior, the day was even warmer and sunnier. As the two straw-capped companions again strolled arm in arm across the Zócalo, Frances was even more enthralled with the vibrant scene that, as if in a movie, had burst into life since they entered the Cathedral.

Chapter Eight

A few blocks beyond the other side of the Zócalo, they arrived at the unadorned stone complex of the Convent of San Jeronimo, a stark contrast with the grand Baroque cathedral at the western side.

Thanks to Juan Carlos, Frances had been introduced to Sor Juana de la Cruz via the brilliant biography written by Mexican Nobel laureate Octavio Paz. According to Paz, Sor Juana, born in Mexico in 1648, a half century after Bruno's martyrdom, also had been drawn to the writings of the ancient philosopher Hermes Trismegistus. That a seventeenth century cloistered Mexican nun was even familiar with what she identified as the Hermetic tradition astounded Frances, and when she read the Paz book, she glowed with added pleasure derived from his fulsome praise of her own unique scholarship regarding Bruno.

Furthermore, she strongly identified with the *religiosa,* who had refused an arranged marriage and instead chose to enter a convent where she could pursue the life of the mind. Many years ago, Frances too had declined an offer of marriage and dedicated herself to her studies and writing. While she did not consider herself an ardent feminist like Sor Juana, Frances also was more or less an auto-didactic and shared with the Mexican nun a voracious appetite for reading and love of learning. In a way, she further realized, the hallowed Warburg Institute was her own convent, since the musty library on Woburn Square had been an intellectual and spiritual haven for nearly half a century. Of course, unlike martyred Sor Juana, who had been punished for her nonconformity by having her books taken away, Frances had been nurtured at the Warburg Institute. Except for physical torture and death by fire, she could hardly imagine a worse punishment than losing her books!

Yet while Juana was dead of plague at the young age of forty-seven, at seventy-five, Frances marveled she still was eager to explore new paths, as exemplified by her recent fascination with Tarot and now most unexpectedly the impact of the Hermetic tradition in Mexico.

A frequent visitor to the convent's reconstituted collection of Sor Juana's Hermetic library, Juan Carlos had arranged a meeting with Frances and the Sisters of San Jeronimo. Certainly, he strategized, it was a match made in Heaven, and initiating the visit to Mexico of a renowned British scholar of the Hermetic tradition wouldn't harm pending endorsements of his dissertation. His focus on the influence of the Hermetic tradition in Latin America had led him to the Warburg Institute and Dame Frances Yates.

In heavily accented but fluent formal English, the Abadesa Teresa Montoya, leader of the dwindling order of nuns, greeted Frances at the entrance to the convent by bowing graciously and kissing her hand.

"My dear Dama Francesca, what a tremendous honor and profound pleasure it is to welcome you to San Jeronimo, the home of sainted Sor Juana! Each of your brilliant books has been added to her library and studied with great appreciation by my *sorjuanistas*, as I call them. Indeed, each of us is most anxious to discuss the Hermetic tradition with you the day after tomorrow. Perhaps in the meantime I can accompany you and your colleagues on a tour of the convent and Sor Juana's chamber, where her famous portrait hangs."

Also in her seventies with straight, gray hair pulled back from a high, noble forehead into a simple bun at the nape of her neck, Abadesa Teresa wore a simple, black, long-sleeved shin-length cotton dress with black stockings and sturdy black shoes. Her hair was covered with a short, white linen veil that just touched her shoulders, framing her bronzed complexion and deep, dark eyes circled with wire-rimmed glasses. Somewhat stocky, except for her dark eyes, the Abadesa reminded Elizabeth of a clerical version of Dame Frances. A faint whiff of lily hovered about her.

Chapter Nine

Long before she met her in the Convent, Abadesa Teresa Montoya felt as if she knew Dame Frances Yates. When she first read the Spanish translation of *Giordano Bruno and the Hermetic Tradition*, Sor Teresa felt as if she had encountered a soulmate. Now she had two: Sor Juana de la Cruz was the other.

That a contemporary like-minded and spiritually-attuned Anglican woman should identify and unravel the teachings of another earlier mystical martyr, Giordano Bruno, implied to Teresa she and Frances shared a similar worldview with universal appeal. Beneath the ancient ritual she cherished and symbolized her own spiritual transformation, Teresa identified with the Hermetic tradition, as articulated by Frances.

Like Frances, Teresa was born in a time of political turmoil, the Mexican Revolution of 1910, and like Frances whose only brother died in World War I, she too lost a revered older brother in the subsequent violence. A fervent democrat and patriot, young Geofredo Montoya had joined the forces of the Revolution. The impact of these deaths on both families was devastating. Teresa's father, night manager of a hotel in Coyoacan, assuaged the loss of his only son with alcohol and spent little time at home where, like Frances Yates in England, Teresa found solace and escape from the gloom and loneliness in books. When Teresa discovered the poetry of Sor Juana de la Cruz on the shelf beside her mother's bed, she was enraptured, and when she saw her mother had folded the page at a poem titled "You Foolish Men," she was mesmerized:

You foolish men who lay
The guilt on women,
Not seeing you're the cause
Of the very thing you blame;
If you invite their disdain
With measureless desire
Why wish they will behave
If you incite to ill.

Unlike Frances, Teresa Montoya was an ardent feminist. Angry at the men of both sides of the fighting who had taken her son away, her mother Carlota railed against patriarchy—in politics and especially the Church, whose priests dared to preach to her Geofredo's death was God's will.

In spite of the loss of their son and his revolutionary cause, the Montoya family found solace in the Church's ancient rituals and continued to attend weekly Mass on Sundays and Holy Days, and since it was the only adequate education for girls, Teresa attended school at the Convento of San Jeronimo, where very soon her intelligence was recognized and encouraged by the nuns. By the time she was in her early teens, Teresa was fluent in Latin and English, and including Cervantes and Shakespeare and every word by Sor Juana, had read every book in the convent library. After school she assisted the nuns with administrative chores in the library and office and quickly was appreciated for her grace and efficiency.

When it was first proposed to her mother Teresa might become a novitiate, not surprisingly, Carlota balked. Yet as she considered alternatives for her talented daughter, respectable marriage (with or without love) and ensuing numerous children who later might be taken from her by war and illness, ironically, she came to appreciate the freedoms convent life afforded women in conservative Mexico. As for sixteen-year old Teresa, there was no second thought. The mindless tedium of managing a household for an autocratic husband along with a passel of unruly children held no appeal. Above all there was the paradigm of Sor Juana de la Cruz, who had rejected an arranged prestigious marriage to pursue the life of the mind. Very few of the so-called attractions of secular life such as clothes, parties, and movies appealed to her. On her seventeenth birthday, after several solitary hours spent contemplating the Cabrera portrait in Juana's chambers, she too decided to spend the rest of her life in contemplation, surrounded by books.

Of course, not all hours in the Convent could be spent in the library or chapel. Always there was work to be done to keep the community intact—especially in light of the fact fewer and fewer young Mexican women were attracted to a cloistered life. Periodically, as a result, the Church hierarchy threatened to shutter San Jeronimo's doors—until the publication and translation of the Paz biography of Sor Juana, which garnered universal acclaim. Along with flourishing tourism, as more and more North Americans discovered the warmth and charms of Mexico, curious scholars explored and delighted in the remarkable and heretofore underappreciated convent library.

While she pursued her religious studies, thoughtfully her predecessor Abadesa Concepcion assigned Teresa to the library, where the novitiate immersed herself in Sor Juana's aura. Eventually, as she studied incessantly and matured, Teresa was appointed assistant then head librarian. With clearer understanding of its scope and context, Teresa suggested to the Abadesa to keep the collection relevant and appealing to scholars it be updated judiciously and expanded with relevant volumes, such as the Paz biography. Another by an English scholar named Frances Yates also was recommended by a history professor from the university who had studied at the Warburg Institute. Thus, Giordano Bruno and the Hermetic tradition were integrated into the world of Sor Juana de la Cruz. As Teresa's spiritual life enhanced exponentially, she was convinced martyred Sor Juana and Giordano Bruno were kindred spirits.

Chapter Ten

The group's first stop was the stark ground floor stucco chapel, where immediately Frances' eyes were riveted not on the simple altar but instead on a colorful painting hanging on the white wall between two large rectangular windows. Noticing Frances staring at the painting, Elizabeth followed her and soon too was transfixed. In a gilded frame no more than six by eight feet wide and high, a recumbent and decidedly effeminate Christ reclined provocatively on a bed of red and white flowers.

"Can you please tell us something about this remarkable painting, Abadesa?" Frances inquired.

"Indeed, Dama Francesca, it is *El Divino Esposo*, one of the two works housed in the Convent by Miguel Cabrera, one of Mexico's greatest artists," the Abadesa informed them. "The other is his famous portrait of Sor Juana, which hangs in her chambers upstairs. This painting was created for the *monjitos* to enhance their contemplation and devotion to Christ as sacred husband. As you may know, nuns are accustomed to believe themselves brides of Christ, and this painting has been interpreted as a portrayal of Christ awaiting his bride."

Taking a few moments to absorb the image, Frances exclaimed, "How extraordinary!" Glancing aside at Elizabeth, she lowered her voice and murmured, "Surely something else is going on here, wouldn't you say?"

With raised eyebrows and wide eyes, Elizabeth whispered, "Clearly."

For this remarkable Christ with a beguiling expression on his face and a flowing azure blue wrap had slightly bulging breasts and a soft, fleshy effeminate hand resting on his pubic area. As if nursing, a sweet young lamb rested its head on Christ's foot. Quietly the two astounded visitors agreed to a later discussion of the remarkable portrayal, although simultaneously both were reminded of another androgynous Christ with breasts depicted in the Marseilles Tarot.

The Divine Spouse by Miguel Cabrera

"Christ reclining on a bed of flowers..." Frances pondered. "I wonder if Cabrera is known at the Warburg, and if not, how is it possible a handful of nuns in a convent in Mexico City could be more attuned to ancient pre-patriarchal myths than some of the finest scholars in Europe?"

At the top of a narrow stone stairway, Sor Juana's chamber was more spacious and gracious than Frances ever imagined a nun's quarters could be. With high ceilings and a balcony with a delicate wrought iron railing, the chamber consisted of a parlor lined floor to ceiling with bookshelves and a simple, stark bedroom with a window overlooking the courtyard garden, which Sor Juana could access privately through a narrow door. A small closet housed a metal tub for private bathing. With a gilded Crucifix hanging above, a carved mahogany *prie-dieu* stood in one corner of the parlor, while a replica of Juana's telescope, confiscated by the Inquisition, was placed in another corner across the chamber. The telescope had enabled Sor Juana to confirm Copernicus's heliocentric worldview, which threatened the geocentric fixed order on which Church hierarchy was founded. In the center of the chamber, a large, simple wood table afforded adequate place for reading and writing. Indeed, if she had been a *religiosa*, Frances imagined, it was an apartment that suited her own habits, and she could imagine herself working there. Yet her deep, if unorthodox faith notwithstanding, she often wondered whether she could or would have had the courage to resist unto death the forces of the Inquisition, as both Bruno and Sor Juan had so valiantly. To prolong his torture, Bruno had been burned with green wood and how stunning Juana had been forced to sign a renunciation of her writings, as she did with her own blood, declaring herself, "I, the Worst of All!"

Over the fireplace Cabrera's riveting portrait of Sor Juana commanded the room.

Portrait of Sor Juana de la Cruz by Miguel Cabrera

Sitting at the table before her books and a clock with her hand on an open book, Sor Juana gazed directly at the viewer. With wing-like sleeves, her elegant white habit trimmed in light blue, rested on a small Oriental rug at her feet. Enormous rosary beads floated from her neck to knees and, framing her face, a black scapular covered her head and fell over her breast on which a large round escutcheon with a scene of the Nativity rested.

"Certainly," Frances surmised, "no serious scholar could work at her desk with such obtrusive ornamentation." What, therefore, was Cabrera's message and the meaning of this painting, and why once again did the scene remind her of Tarot, which she now readily acknowledged she now saw everywhere?

Although there were few remaining followers, somehow the Sisters of San Jeronimo had managed to survive the Inquisition's purge of the convent's library in the 1690s when Sor Juana's telescope and library were scoured from the premises. Soon after she was ordered to a dispensary to care for other nuns who were ill with the plague, Juana too succumbed and died in 1695 at age 43.

How tragic, Frances noted, worlds apart, two fervent advocates of a true universal church with an underlying message of tolerance and acceptance should be martyred at the same time, and how much more she needed to learn about Latin American history! First and foremost, how did the Hermetic tradition find its way to the Americas—or, she discerned with astonishment, was it possible because of its inherent universality, two brilliant mystics an ocean apart arrived independently at the same conviction?

"What on earth was going on in Mexico in the 1600's?" she said, turning from the remarkable painting Frances posed to Elizabeth. "I am embarrassed to admit until I saw the portrait of Sor Juana on the cover of the Paz book, I had never heard of Miguel Cabrera."

"Nor have I, Dame Frances, even though I have visited Mexico several times," Elizabeth confessed. Then addressing her colleagues, she vowed, "Embarrassed to admit until this trip I have not taken into account how little we in America know about Mexico and Latin American history and art. In the future I intend to remedy my ignorance."

Beaming, the Abadesa responded, "My friends, I am so very pleased Sor Juana's spirit speaks also to you. Every day and each time I enter her chamber,

I am inspired by her notions of spiritual universality, the life of the mind, and equality for women and men."

Enveloped by the hallowed atmosphere and aware of the bold ideas fostered here, before leaving the chamber Frances placed her open palm against the large, carved stone embedded into the brick wall and dedicated to Juana's memory. Then, as she did whenever she stood before Bruno's statue in the Campo dei Fiori, aware of the remarkable confluence of events that brought the twentieth century British champion of an Italian martyr to far away Mexico, she said a silent prayer of gratitude to the martyred *religiosa*.

As the visitors descended the narrow stone stairway and approached the front door of the convent, the Abadesa gently shook the hand of each guest, thanked them for their visit, and reiterated how much she and the other *religiosas* were anticipating Frances's presentation on Wednesday.

Chapter Eleven

Captivated and overwhelmed by their entrée into another time and place, the four comrades bid farewell to the gracious Abadesa and unanimously expressed their gratitude for her hospitality. Yet by the time they again reached the Zócalo, it became apparent their initial reactions varied. Justifiably Juan Carlos was pleased with his negotiations that had brought esteemed Dame Frances Yates to Mexico. Impressed by the unique experience and the doors it had opened in her mind, Elizabeth was eager for further adventures, while Drummond in turn was energized by her enthusiasm. Yet captivated and stimulated by her first-hand encounter with Sor Juana, Frances was virtually wilting before their eyes. Undoubtedly, she also was suffering aftershocks from the previous night's partying.

Appraising the situation, *sotto voce* Elizabeth consulted with Juan Carlos; quickly they devised alternative plans for the group's afternoon activities.

"Dama Francesca," Juan Carlos suggested, "Perhaps you have noticed the Zócalo now is much quieter than it was when we entered the Convent," as indeed it was.

"Why, yes," Frances glanced about. "Why is that? Has something happened?"

"It is because here in Mexico we have the tradition of *siesta* or 'rest' during the warmest hours of the day," her host informed her. "Perhaps that idea appeals to you as well? If so, I suggest we return to the Majestic for some refreshment and then you can rest before dinner at another of my favorite bistros."

"What a marvelous idea," Frances, who felt she was on the verge of collapse, exclaimed gratefully. "If only instead of tea we had such a civilized custom in Europe!"

After a sidebar and assured Frances would be shepherded by Juan Carlos, whom they thanked profusely for a fascinating morning, Elizabeth and Drummond inquired whether he could recommend a nearby bistro for lunch. Cordially Frances and Juan Carlos wished the newlyweds a *"Buen viaje!"* as they strolled toward the far side of the Zócalo.

"We must keep in mind they are on their honeymoon," Frances noted. Halfway across the Zócalo on their way to the Majestic, she remembered and informed Juan Carlos of an impending emergency: Her supply of Woodbines was running low!

Unflappable, her young host assured her, *"No es problema, Dama Francesca,* some Deliciados—how do you say—will do the trick!"

Stopping at a kiosk beneath the arcade of the Zócalo, Dame Frances Yates made her first purchase in Mexico using pesos Elizabeth had exchanged for her to have in her purse. Relieved, she admired the handsome white box with its bold lion, and lighting up immediately, exhaled hearty Mexican smoke with a sigh of relief and satisfaction. Finally, they reached the hotel and once again entered the Terraza where Frances Yates fell in love. His name was Jésus Rodruguez. At the entrance to the restaurant, he greeted them with fluent melodic English and escorted them to a small table by the open windows where he held her chair and made certain Frances was safely and comfortably seated.

"Por favor, Profesora...."

So, he too knew who she was. *How gracious these Mexicans are!* she marveled.

Very soon and over the next few days, Jésus, who somehow seemed able to anticipate and appreciate her culinary tastes and every need, became a virtual knight in shining armor. Legendary Jésus had been a fixture at the Majestic for nearly twenty years and was known to a worldwide cast of devoted clients. Beginning as a busboy when he was sixteen and needing to earn money to support his widowed mother and siblings, he had studied assiduously to improve his English and manners, rising to become headwaiter at the renowned hotel. Over the years, Jésus had encountered prime ministers and movie stars, but now an elderly and disheveled British scholar seemed to capture his heart—perhaps because she reminded him of his own dear departed *abuela*.

Since breakfast bunches of fragrant fresh roses in pottery vases had been placed on every table. Immediately, along with an ashtray, a tall glass pitcher of ice cold water flavored with floating slices of fresh lemon and lime appeared on the table, and their glasses instantly filled. "

Wonderful!" Frances proclaimed as she gulped and finally came up for air.

Magically a straw basket lined with a red cotton napkin and spilling over with large blue chips accompanied by a bowl filled with a light green creamy substance arrived.

"What is this, Juan Carlos? What makes it green?" she inquired.

"It is guacamole, which is made from avocado, Dama Francesca, and it is not at all spicy. Please try some," he urged, as he dipped a warm chip into the green paste and handed it to her. "I think you will like it."

In all likelihood because the consistency resembled her beloved English custards, Frances's first taste of the exotic native fruit was divine, and hastily she assembled another scoop, then a third. Noting her obvious zeal, Jésus reappeared with menus as well as suggestions.

"Perhaps a thick hot bean soup accompanied by a salad of fresh tomato, cucumber and cilantro, along with a plate of warm tortillas would please the professor?"

Grateful to Jésus for his thoughtfulness, Juan Carlos opted for heartier fare of a thick chopped *biftek* sandwich on a grainy bun smothered in a spicy sauce of chili peppers that made even his eyes water. For dessert, Jésus proffered a plate of freshly baked chewy coconut cookies with cups of fresh pineapple chunks and bright red sweet Mexican strawberries. Lighting her second Deliciado, Frances relished the comforting meal and the devoted attention of two such solicitous and mannerly courtiers. At the same time, she was both refreshed and terribly fatigued.

Thanking and bidding farewell to Jésus, who bowed with a gracious, "*Un placer, Profesora*," she accepted the strong arm of Juan Carlos, who escorted her to sala 535, where she quickly disrobed, crawled between fresh sheets, and slept deeply and blissfully for the rest of the afternoon of her first full day in Mexico.

Chapter Twelve

Rather than lingering over a leisurely lunch, sure to slow them down with too much good food and sangria, and anxious to see the Rivera murals, Elizabeth and Drummond decided instead to dine on a bench at the bustling Zócalo. With her pocket dictionary in hand and a few words of hesitant Spanish, Elizabeth managed to order two spicy beef tacos and cold *cervesas*, which they devoured while watching parade before them the vibrant panoply of Mexico's cultural complexities, personified by indigenous, mestizos, African-Americans and criollos, along with tourists from around the world.

"Thank God for paper napkins!" Elizabeth laughed as thick salsa oozed between her fingers.

"And thank God for cold beer!" Drummond added. "This salsa business could bring a grown man to his knees!"

"Man up, Stuart!" Elizabeth laughed as hand in spicy hand they headed to the National Palace.

The murals were stunning. On a balcony surrounding the courtyard and soaring above the spectators, they had been created in the 1930s following the Mexican Revolution. The riotous masterpiece depicted the history of Mexico since ancient times through the Revolution of 1910 with portraits of Zapata and Juarez. Saturated with Rivera's fervent leftist politics, scenes included dictators, indigenous women being ravaged by Spanish soldiers, and sacred indigenous texts burned by Jesuit priests. More effectively than any dreary textbook, Elizabeth opined to Drummond, the human faces of the murals were a statement against colonial oppression, exemplified by the red banner proclaiming, *"Tierra y Libertad!"*

In the context of Russian oppression and the Cold War, Drummond thought Rivera's adulation of communism naïve and irresponsible. At the same time, the thought of ancient texts being destroyed by the Spaniards offended him deeply.

"What's been lost?" he shook his head, contemplating once again why and what about ancient knowledge could be so threatening to Church authorities.

Including last year's episode at the Warburg, stealing and destroying books were among the most senseless crimes he had investigated over the years. Certainly it was all about money and power. Soberly and thoughtfully, the couple returned to the Majestic where, with a pitcher of cold sangria and a lilting Marquez danzon playing softly in the background, they sat on the terrace and contemplated how in just a few hours in Mexico City their minds and worldview were expanding, as their newly forged bond grew stronger and deeper.

Chapter Thirteen

For their second dinner in Mexico City and, it turned out, a fitting sequel to the Rivera murals, Juan Carlos escorted his guests to the wood-paneled La Opera Bar, established in 1876 by two French sisters in the Centro Historico on the *avenida* Cinco de Mayo, which Juan Carlos informed them commemorates the date of the Mexican army's victory over the French invaders at the Battle of Puebla in 1862. Contrary to the common assumption, the date did *not* mark Mexico's independence from Spain, which had been achieved a half-century earlier. Legend held several obvious holes in the Bar's very high ceiling were the result of gunshots fired by infamous bandito Pancho Villa during the great Mexican Revolution of 1910.

Greeted by a gracious hostess dressed in colorful *china poblana* costume worn by stylish Mexican women and favored by Frida Kahlo, they were seated in an ornate, high-backed, polished wooden booth, cushioned in worn, red velvet that complemented the ornate, red, patterned wallpaper and refurbished gaslights. Lilting folk music played in the background as they reviewed their first full day in Mexico City.

Once again Juan Carlos opened the evening's menu negotiations, "Tonight, *mis amigos*, I might suggest we drink sangria—perhaps a pitcher for the table."

"Excellent choice, Juan Carlos," Elizabeth affirmed. "I'm sure it would please Dame Frances as well."

Like her colleagues, Elizabeth, who had savored the sweet drink on her previous visits, was concerned Frances not overindulge once again this evening.

"The name 'sangria' is taken from the Spanish word for' "blood' (*sangre*)," Juan Carlos informed his guests, "and according to the legend, the sweet, red wine punch laced with fresh orange juice and chopped fruit is thought to resemble the sweetness of Christ's blood."

As they waited for the sangria to arrive, Juan Carlos noted renowned literati who had frequented the famous bar, including Sor Juana's biographer Octavio Paz, Gabriel Garcia Marquez, as well as virtually every president of Mexico Saturated with literature and the arts, the dark wood sanctuary reminded Elizabeth of her favorite Algonquin Hotel.

Was there a Round Table here as well? she wondered, vowing to visit the literary haven in New York City with Stuart and Dame Frances before they returned to London.

Simultaneously Stuart recalled the similar ambience of the Ivy Grill at Convent Garden where he intended to take Elizabeth for cocktails in the near future. In the meantime, the three enchanted visitors concurred there was so much more to learn about Mexico.

When the large glass pitcher, chock full of slices of peaches, oranges, and pineapple arrived, Juan Carlos filled each stemmed glass and raised a toast to "*Amistad!*" and the newlyweds—before sharing his own good news, which he had saved for the appropriate moment. "In the summer I will go to Milano where Petra and I will be married!"

Another former Warburg student, Petra Sfuzzi, worked for Tesoro, the Milan publisher of Frances's books. Charming Petra also had participated in the seminar regarding Tarot while falling deeply in love with the handsome Mexican scholar. After their marriage, he informed them, Petra would move to Mexico City where Tesoro planned to open an affiliate to translate and sell Spanish versions of their publications, while scouting worthwhile Mexican writers as well.

As her companions cheered, Frances beamed, "Once again I am thrilled and claim all of the credit!"

Yet how ironic two perfectly suited couples should evolve from such dour circumstances.

"Talk about resurrection and renewal," she nodded to Elizabeth, a fellow admirer of Joseph Campbell's *Hero with a Thousand Faces*.

"Or perhaps, Dame Frances, one could say it is 'in the cards,'" Elizabeth quickly rejoined.

"*Touché*, my dear," Frances acknowledged, taking her first delightful sip of sweet Mexican punch, while acutely aware that—no matter how enticing—tonight and the rest of her sojourn she must temper her new-found enthusiasm for alcoholic beverages.

"Now please help us again with the menu, Juan Carlos," Elizabeth urged, as she retrieved her tiny yellow pocket Langenscheidt Spanish dictionary from her tote. "I'm famished and can't wait to dive further into our Mexican culinary adventures!"

"Anything *Chamorro* refers to indigenous cuisine, while, *pulpo* is octopus, *caracoles* are snails, and *lengua* is tongue," their host began to explain.

"Oh dear, I'm afraid these options sound much too exotic for me," grimaced Frances, who of course had eaten tongue and, in fact, liked Ruby's bland recipe with cabbage and boiled potatoes. Yet she also recalled an unfortunate encounter last year in London with several fried calamari.

"Perhaps then some corn soup and grilled *biftek* with green *ensalada* with cucumber," Juan Carlos suggested.

"That sounds much better, *gracias*, Juan Carlos," Frances nodded with relief.

It was apparent the astute English scholar had begun to pepper her conversation with a few words of Spanish. Indeed, her dietary qualms notwithstanding, it simultaneously occurred to her three companions that august Dame Frances Yates appeared to be undergoing a transformation in Mexico. Away from the somber Warburg and plied by margaritas and sangria along with warm sunshine, a phenomenon seldom experienced in London, to their delight a light-hearted and charming Frances Yates emerged over every meal. Until now no one other than Frida Hilb, the director of the Warburg, who had traveled with her in her beloved Italy, had caught a glimpse of a less foreboding icon.

At once Elizabeth and Drummond forged boldly ahead into Chamorro pork and octopus, while Juan Carlos selected a crusty white roll stuffed with tender *bacalao a lo tio*, salted cod smothered with pickled chilies and sautéed green onions. While they waited for their entrees, Juan Carlos recommended they share a platter of *huevos diablos* and white *queso* dip with bits of chorizo.

"Deviled eggs," Frances exclaimed, as she eagerly reached for a familiar treat, although these sprinkled with cilantro and just a hint of chili powder tasted so much better than the bland version Ruby prepared for coffee hour at Holy Trinity in Claygate.

For dessert they shared a platter of sweet, doughy churros, served with banana *licuado*. All the while, the party reflected on their stimulating visit to the Convent and insights gained by their personal introduction to Sor Juana de la Cruz and her relationship to the Hermetic tradition. Then, arm in arm, they strolled compatibly and contentedly along charming streets to the Majestic.

Chapter Fourteen

O n Tuesday, Carlos presented his visitors to Mexico's beloved Virgen
de Guadalupe at Tepeyac Hill at the edge of the city where legend proclaimed the Virgin Mother had appeared to indigenous peasant Juan Diego.
As proof to the skeptical Catholic priest who doubted the encounter, the
Blessed Mother had impressed her sacred image on Diego's cape, now enshrined and hung high on a wall at the cathedral built at the site, constructed
atop the remains of a temple dedicated to Corn Mother Goddess Tonantzin.

Our Lady of Guadalupe, Mexico City

With an impressive dome and towers on either side, here was another massive Cathedral. Before it an enormous plaza was teeming with visitors, many murmuring prayers over rosary beads while waiting patiently in a long line to enter the shrine. Wearing colorfully embroidered *huipils*, young indigenous mothers clutched infants wrapped in hand-woven *mantas*. Juan Carlos informed them many of these visitors, called *Guadalupanos*, returned to the shrine again and again.

Through the university, he had managed to obtain passes that enabled them to bypass the line and enter the cathedral by a side door rather than wait outside in the hot sun. Once inside the dark interior, pilgrims were directed to the moving conveyor that transported visitors below the shroud of the Virgen. The electronic sidewalk reminded Elizabeth of similar distasteful contraptions now installed before the Mona Lisa at the Louvre and the Crown Jewels at the Tower of London. It seemed the interest of crowd control, modernity, and efficiency usurped any sense of aesthetics. Concerned especially for Frances's safety, she clasped her mentor's chunky elbow and awkwardly managed to land both of them upright on the relentless albeit slowly moving conveyor. At once she noticed tears were streaming down the cheeks of many of the other pilgrims. As they passed beneath the shroud framed in gold, the first thing Elizabeth observed was this Madonna had indigenous features. At the same time, she noted to Juan Carlos and Frances, Guadalupe recalled the Black Virgin of Monserrat whom she had seen several years ago in the Pyrenees.

"In Catalonia she is seated on a throne high above the altar, and there too there was the same sense of awe and reverence among the pilgrims. In fact, I confess I felt drawn up the steep stairs to rub the orb she holds in her outstretched hand."

"Then perhaps, Elizabeth, it would surprise you to learn there are several Black Madonna's here in Latin America as well."

"That's remarkable!" Elizabeth exclaimed. "Can you believe a colleague in New York once suggested the Monserrat's skin, as well of that of another Black Madonna in Poland, was black because of smoke from all the candles in the cathedral? Yet somehow, he couldn't account for the Virgin's snow-white robe! Please tell us more about the dark Madonnas here!"

As they rambled along on the automated walkway, Juan Carlos told them about the Black Madonna Aparecida of Brazil, where more than in

Mexico, the experience and traditions of African slaves had intersected with indigenous culture.

Yet to Frances's scholarly mind, the immediate and obvious issue was syncretism. When Juan Carlos translated the words beneath Guadalupe's portrait, she was convinced: *I am the Mother of all you who dwell in this land.*

"Extraordinary! Certainly," she observed quietly, "it can't be a coincidence the site of this remarkable relic rests on the tomb of another mother goddess. Truly I am quite overwhelmed by the universality of the prominence of still another female deity."

"Indeed, Dame Frances," Elizabeth affirmed.

"What's more, is it my imagination or does this image remind you, as it does me, of the various portrayals of the powerful women portrayed in the Tarot?"

"Well done, Elizabeth. It seems you have read my mind. Yet here we find ourselves literally a world away from the Middle East where it is believed the cards originated—*if*, that is, we are to believe that is indeed the case. You don't suppose there is some version of the cards here in Mexico as well...."

Despite a lifetime of spiritual yearnings, the omnipresence of a female deity was a phenomenon Frances had overlooked until quite recently.

"Who *is* she?" Frances wondered, reflecting on provocative revelations gleaned from the Tarot and Barbara Walker's *Woman's Encyclopedia of Myths and Secrets,* which with astounding consequences Frida had discovered last year in London.

"If I may, dear ladies," interjected Juan Carlos, who along with Drummond was standing watchfully just behind the two distracted scholars on the moving walkway, "since she incorporates both indigenous and Spanish cultures, it can be said Guadalupe represents the very soul of Mexico. For Mexicans, Tonantzin and the Virgin Mary are one and the same. Tonantzin is Mother Goddess, the Earth Mother, so when the missionaries introduced the indigenous population to the Mother of the Redeemer Christ, they recognized her immediately, and—at least publicly—had no difficulty naming her Mary instead. According to Octavio Paz, the Virgen of Guadalupe shaped our sense of nationhood, since she unified the indigenous who worshipped Tonanztin, along with so-called *criollos* who were pure-bred Spaniards, and *mestizos* who are mixed race Mexicans and the majority of the population today. In fact, during the great Revolution of 1910 she was considered a symbol of Mexican identity and unity."

As they reached the exit of the cathedral and once again joined the throngs at the plaza, they noticed men with the image of Guadalupe tattooed on their arms and chests and vendors selling an array of souvenirs and T-shirts as well. At one booth, Juan Carlos purchased postcards for Frances and Elizabeth.

Frances then surprised her party by asking if they might rejoin the queue and pass once more beneath the remarkable relic. Fascinated with the sacred shroud and the ideals it spawned, she yearned once more to experience the sacred spell cast by Guadalupe. Taking into account her age and Juan Carlos's solicitous request, several unfailingly gracious Mexican pilgrims at the front of the queue permitted them to go ahead and access the conveyor walkway once again.

A half-hour later, a glowing Frances and Juan Carlos emerged from the Cathedral. Wearing baseball hats and chugging bottles of cold *agua fresca de limon* Elizabeth and Drummond waited in the hot sun on a bench near the exit, and they all laughed at Frances's first comment.

"Is it time for siesta?"

Satiated with revelation and insight, Frances was also thoroughly fatigued and very hungry. In light of her presentation tomorrow, she inquired whether they—or at least she—might dine this evening as well at the hotel. New ideas triggered by yesterday's tour of the Convent and today's revelations at Tepeyac percolated in her mind and dining in house would afford her time to revise and polish her remarks.

"*Por favor, mis amigos,*" she urged, "feel free to dine elsewhere. As long as I am cared for by charming Jésus, I am quite comfortable dining alone."

"It's a capital idea, Dame Frances. May we join you?" Drummond came to the rescue.

Pleased with his attentiveness and not minding the idea of a siesta and quiet evening, Elizabeth immediately concurred. At the same time, Juan Carlos admitted to himself he too was tired and relieved not to be responsible for arranging another festive dinner. A taxi took them back to the Majestic for supper. Sensing their fatigue and quietude, Jésus suggested a simple supper of roast capon accompanied by a bottle of La Tente, a lovely rosé wine, followed by cups of tart lemon *sorbete* and warm coconut cookies laced with almonds.

Later in her room, after another soothing tub and somehow managing to shampoo her hair, which she battened down with an army of hairpins,

Frances sat in her worn cotton nightie at a handsome mahogany desk and smoked a Deliciado. Exhaling, she sat back in the cushioned chair and, contemplating new insights gained over her first two days in Mexico, revised her notes for her talk tomorrow in the Convent.

As always, her thoughts turned to her lodestar Bruno.

"What would the great Hermetic think about Sor Juana, I wonder—to say nothing of a blatantly syncretic Virgin Mother?"

Of course, it was purely a rhetorical question that could never be resolved. Yet what would Dame Frances Yates have accomplished if she hadn't employed her vivid historical imagination, a trait she strongly encouraged her students to cultivate? Admittedly hers had been nurtured by an unorthodox education and decades at the Warburg that afforded the freedom to scour literature and art as well as tedious conventional texts.

"But despite his nonconformity, might not...would Bruno have been able to accept the notion of a Great Mother? Or, like most clerics of his time, was his worldview too steeped in patriarchy to incorporate such a radical concept? And even if he had, it is difficult to contemplate the Inquisition's heightened response to this added transgression! Except to torture him further or somehow burn him even more slowly, what more could they have done to him? How could it have been any worse?"

With a bright blue plastic pen stamped "Majestic" that would become a treasured souvenir, she inserted new thoughts into her lecture notes.

"It is fascinating to me within a mere half-century, here in Mexico we encountered another martyr to more or less the same 'heresies' [use fingers to mimic quotation marks] and this one advocated by a woman! Coupled with my visit yesterday to the cathedral at Tepeyac, the decided femininity of Mexican spirituality is fascinating."

Chapter Fifteen

At nine the next morning Frances and Juan Carlos were greeted at the door of the convent by Abadesa Teresa who thanked Juan Carlos for delivering Frances.

"*Muchas gracias, caro* Juan Carlos. Perhaps you can call for Dama Francesca at two after our service and discussion and a simple *comida*; then she can return to her hotel for siesta."

"*Un placer, Abadesa*," Juan Carlos bowed discreetly. While he yearned to witness the event, he realized the ambiance would be tainted by the presence of a solitary male participant.

Holding her hand, the Abbess escorted Frances to the chapel, where the other nuns, eagerly awaiting, were seated in a circle of straight-backed wooden chairs. When Frances and the Abadesa appeared at the doorway, each nun immediately stood and gently applauded. To accommodate Frances by taking into account her age and any lingering jet lag, the Abbess had postponed the usual time for the daily congregation from seven to nine o'clock. One by one the Abbess presented Dame Frances to each of the convent's few remaining *monjas*, Gertrudis, Rosa, Susana, Maria, Lucia, Letitia, Carmela, and Angela, who cradled a guitar. Entering the circle, Frances exchanged gentle handshakes with each *religiosa* before joining the Abadesa at one of two empty chairs. Surveying the circle, Frances noted–with the exception of two younger women who appeared to be identical—each of the nuns was mature—none seeming younger than forty or fifty years of age. As she surmised, the cloistered life held little appeal to more recent generations. Yet, as Juan Carlos had informed her, the Sisters of San Jeronimo were ardent social activists, working among the aged, impoverished, and indigenous communities of Mexico City.

"Usually, Dama Francesca," the Abadesa informed her, "we sing a hymn and then sit quietly for contemplative time before the Eucharist, after which we eagerly anticipate sharing your insights and enhancing our understanding regarding the Hermetic tradition. Of course, each of us has read your great book about Bruno!"

Enormously flattered, Frances nodded and responded, "It would be an honor, Abadesa,"

Whereupon Sor Angela began to strum her guitar and the gentle voices of the nuns blended in harmony. Unexpectedly, the sweet sounds brought tears to Frances's eyes. Although sung in Spanish, the simple hymn was familiar:

I, the God of sea and sky, I have heard my people cry. All who dwell in dark and sin my hand will save...

At the refrain in her smoke-damaged, slightly off-key voice, softly in English, Frances joined the refrain, as bilingual Sor Susana met her eyes with a smile and joined her.

Here I am, God. Is it I, God? I have heard you calling in the night. I will go, God, if you lead me. I will hold your people in my heart...

Then as a veil of silence descended over group, Frances closed her eyes and marveled at the chain of remarkable events that had led her to a colonial convent halfway round the world in Mexico...the dreadful events last year at the Warburg, which notably had led also to insights regarding Tarot, along with new friendships among her accomplished students such as Juan Carlos who had introduced Frances to Sor Juana and the influence of the Hermetic tradition in Colonial Mexico.

"How remarkable!" as her thoughts veered to the legendary nun who had spent her life in this very convent, surrounded by her books and scientific instruments: There was so much more to learn, and perhaps even write, about Juana.

After twenty minutes or so, with outstretched palms, the Abadesa broke the silence and invited the women to join hands and exchange peace.

"*Paz, querida Dama Francesca,*" she said first, turning to her right to embrace Frances on both cheeks. "We are so grateful you are here."

Moved once again to tears, Frances then turned to her right to greet young Sor Rosa who warmly pressed her hand and said, "*Paz y bienvenida, Dama Francesca.*"

When Sor Susana stood to deliver the first reading, Frances was stunned to see her holding a copy of the *Gnostic Gospels*, which Frances had devoured when, creating an uproar, they were published in 1979 by American scholar Elaine Pagels. Thoroughly bilingual, Sor Susana had been asked to read from the *Gospel of Mary*, as—first in English, then Spanish—she accomplished flawlessly. Although familiar, when Frances heard Peter's questions regarding Mary Magdalene, the first person to encounter risen Christ, she was taken aback:

"Did the Savior really speak with a woman without our knowledge and not openly? Are we to listen to her? Did he prefer her to us?

"Just what's going on in the Convent?" she reflected.

At the end of the reading, the Abadesa delivered a brief homily. Speaking in English for Frances's benefit, while Sor Susana translated into Spanish for her colleagues, the Abadesa extolled and gave thanks for the insights and bold feminine voices of the past, including several whose names were familiar to Frances: Julian of Norwich, Hildegard of Bingen, Margery Kempe, Catherine of Siena, Therese of Lisieux, and Latina Rosa of Lima.

When she had finished her brief prepared remarks, she added, "Now, Dama Francesca, in the spirit of sainted Maria Magdalena and Sor Juana and regardless of their denomination, all guests are invited to share the Eucharist at San Jeronimo. Won't you please join us?"

"It would be an honor," Frances immediately responded, while wondering when a priest would appear to conduct the service.

To her astonishment, Abbess Teresa rose from her chair, approached the tapestry-covered table, bowed, and began to prepare the Elements, the bread and wine followers believed would be transformed by the priest into the Body and Blood of Christ. Stunned, Frances realized the Abbess herself was about to conduct the ancient ritual, which she cherished. Indeed, something quite remarkable was taking place in the Convent of San Jeronimo!

"A woman Magus!" she marveled.

Since her engagement with Tarot, she was convinced during the Eucharist both Anglican and Catholic priests were performing the role of Magus or Magician, transforming the Elements, as represented on card number I of each and every deck of Tarot. Yet although she still was acclimating herself to women priests in the Anglican service and was aware women presided over the ritual at meetings of the Friends of Miriam, a dissident group of Catholics in London to which Frida belonged, never before had Frances ever participated in their services. How she wished her dear colleague Frida Hilb and the Sisters of Miriam could be here! For years the group of feminist Catholics had participated in the Women's Ordination Conference, which advocated for Catholic women priests.

That the movement could also take root in archly Catholic Latin America was a revelation.

"Yet now that I think about it, isn't it possible and even likely Sor Juana also presided over the Eucharist in the Convent, or perhaps, as Frida has done, administered the Elements to herself? In any event, certainly Sor Juana is with us in spirit."

Even though conducted in Spanish, Frances acknowledged the Abadesa meticulously performed the ancient and universal ritual, carefully breaking several thin, crisp wafers in the silver dish into just the right number of pieces for each communicant after pouring sweet red wine from a heavy silver pitcher into an ornate silver goblet, all the while gently waving her aged but graceful hands over each to effect the transformation.

As she knelt on a worn needlepoint cushion before the communion table and the sweet wine and crisp wafer melded in her mouth, the lifelong devout Anglican for whom the ritual was a metaphor for spiritual transformation, was aware her feelings regarding the unique experience had swerved from apprehension to elation. Once again and now in a convent in Mexico of all places, she felt herself transported to a place of inner peace. Never again would she question the Eucharist was a universal ritual with ancient roots.

Along with the others, Frances returned to her seat and sat quietly reflecting while happening to notice one empty chair. Apparently one of the nuns had disappeared and not participated in the ritual.

Which woman was it? she wondered, as she tried to recall their names and faces, but since they were dressed identically in habits with heads covered and more or less of a certain age, the exercise was futile and in the current context seemed irrelevant. Instead, finding herself halfway round the world from her beloved Holy Trinity at Claygate, Frances was overwhelmed by the reach of the Universal Church for which she yearned and fervently believed was the essence of Bruno's healing message. Furthermore, as a result of her recent revelations regarding Tarot, she was convinced notions of the Universal Church reached beyond the Judeo-Christian tradition.

Still, a feminist perspective in archly Catholic Mexico belied any and all preconceptions (or were they prejudices?) she had regarding Catholic countries. Was it really that surprising, however, the yearnings of the Women's Ordination Conference were also experienced here in Mexico, where a syncretized Holy Mother was virtually woven into the national character? Perhaps even more so within this small but valiant cadre of devout women keeping vigil over the legacy of martyred Sor Juana de la Cruz?

The service closed with a prayer, which the nuns recited by heart and thoughtfully Sor Susana had handwritten in English on a sheet of paper she shared with Frances:

Our Mother, Our Father, on earth and in heaven blessed be your compassionate presence, Your images and names. Fill us with your Spirit, Show us the wisdom of Your ways. Forgive us. Teach us to forgive. Shield us from temptation and protect us from all harm. Prevent us from hurting the ones we love, from injuring others in word or in deed, from desecrating our planet. Thank you for the teachings of Sor Juana and the presence today of Dama Francesca and be with us and within us now and always. Amen

Chapter Sixteen

From the chapel the small cadre walked a few steps to the nearby refectory where they were greeted graciously by Sores Maria and Lucia. Except for the high ceiling, the unadorned beige walls momentarily reminded Frances of the basement tearoom at the Warburg, where she dined most days when she was in London. A long wooden table was covered with a soft linen cloth hemmed, the Abadesa recounted, with colorful indigenous flowers embroidered centuries ago by earlier residents of the Convent. Further, she noted, the nuns were vegetarians and grew most of their own food in the garden within the convent courtyard. Inwardly Frances, a devout culinary conservative, cringed.

"Dear Lord, what on earth will we be eating?"

The simple lunch was surprisingly delicious. Deep, heavy pottery bowls of hearty bean soup served with warm tortillas and mounds of newly discovered and divine guacamole, were followed by cups of sliced tart mango (another revelation!) and sweet banana with freshly baked chocolate cookies and fragile antique china cups of hot, fragrant hibiscus tea.

Although she yearned for a Deliciado, Frances noted, "I must remember to take some hibiscus tea home to Ruby."

After the luncheon, which pleasantly energized rather than enervating Frances, the group decamped to the library. With somber lighting, the spacious two-story space rimmed by a balcony, crammed with additional volumes immediately reminded Frances of the reading room of the Warburg. In one corner a huge antique globe of the world was encircled with heavy brass rings engraved with diagrams of various planets that could be rotated to account for the movement of the heavens in a geocentric world. Of course, with her telescope Sor Juana would have perceived a very different concept of the universe that threatened Church hierarchy, which was based on a fixed sun-centered and finite universe. Frances recalled Frida had reported seeing a similar globe in King Philip II's library at Escorial.

Along with her cordial assistant Sor Susana and the Abadesa, waspish librarian Sor Carmela, led Frances on a brief tour of the rare collection. It seemed to Frances that Carmela was impatient for the visit to end and also earlier that morning may have swallowed a Mexican lemon. At the same time, she realized Carmela was the nun missing from the Eucharist. Perhaps the sourpuss came ahead to prepare for the tour. In any event, it was apparent Sor Carmela would prefer to be elsewhere.

Not surprisingly, the Convent's catalog was much more straightforward than the convoluted system devised by Aby Warburg and organized according to his unique worldview. As Sor Carmela related, copies of as many volumes of Sor Juana's own collection were once again reassembled on the shelves, along with noteworthy recent additions which, she noted, now included several of Frances's books. Expressing her satisfaction and gratitude, along the way Frances also noted the Paz biography of Sor Juana (in both Spanish and English translation). Several other titles with which she was familiar and pleased to see as well included Joseph Campbell's *Hero*, Jonathan Spence on Matteo Ricci, the Jesuit priest, who probed spiritual mysteries in the Far East; American Elaine Pagels's ground-breaking *Gnostic Gospels*, which had explored the treasures discovered in the 1940s at Nag Hamadi; and even, to her amazement, Michael Dummett on Tarot, which had unleashed the terrible turmoil at the Warburg. All in all, in a very confined space, it was a remarkably sophisticated collection. Apparently, researchers, such as Juan Carlos and other visitors, along with several of the resident nuns, read English.

Chapter Seventeen

Although she would have relished time to linger among the intriguing volumes, a few moments later Frances was seated at one end of a long wooden table in the center of the library with the Abadesa at the other end and four *monjas* on each side.

"Dama Francesca," the Abadesa began, "we have read your great work and would be grateful if you could explain the significance of *la tradicion hermetica* and especially what it means to you personally. Then since our English is flawed, Sor Susana, who is a graduate of the University of San Diego in California, will translate for those of us who are less fluent."

Halfway down the table on the right, Sor Susana, a petite, dark-skinned *religiosa* once again smiled at Frances and nodded her head. "*Por favor* speak slowly, Dama Francesca," she urged.

Although she was a deliberate (some said ponderous) speaker, Frances appreciated the request, "Please let me know if I am speaking too quickly, Sor Susana, but first, if I may, tell me how your congregation came to embrace feminist theology, lately a topic that interests me enormously. Of course, since we are in the spiritual home of revered Sor Juana, I can't think of a more appropriate venue."

As her flock turned toward her, Abadesa Teresa flushed slightly and smiled softly while acknowledging the query. "Admittedly, Dama Francesca, to avoid any possible discomfort, I could and should have cautioned you regarding our practices, but given Bruno's message of universality and your noble dissemination of his message, I took the decision to proceed without—how do you say?—fanfare. And if we—more specifically I—have inflicted any discomfort upon you, I sincerely apologize."

"Quite the contrary, Abesada, I am tremendously flattered," Frances immediately assuaged her hostess. "As it happens, recent events in London have opened my eyes, heart, and soul to the presence of the Great Mother. As a result, my spiritual life has been enhanced enormously and today even more so by your ritual.

Visibly, the Abadesa sighed with relief. "Unfortunately, I am sorry to say our practices must be kept secret from Cardinal Mendoza, who, to say the least, is not at all sympathetic toward our feminist worldview. Indeed, if ever revealed, we fear the Vatican once again would purge San Jeronimo! Nonetheless out of esteem for your ecumenical writings, we decided to have faith in the Great Mother's compassion and share our unorthodox ritual with you."

As always, the horrors of Bruno's brutal martyrdom and the ferocity of the Inquisition flashed through Frances's vivid imagination.

"Rest assured your secret is safe with me. Even though they evolved quite late in life, thanks to my newfound revelations, my own faith has been deepened and enhanced by awareness of a feminist theology."

"Oh, Dama Francesca, I am so happy!" young Sor Rosa, whose sweet face was aglow with excitement and pleasure, exclaimed spontaneously.

So young, Frances observed, *What could have drawn her to this cloistered life? She couldn't be more than twenty-five and everyone else here is old enough to be her mother, the Abadesa even her grandmother.*

Virtually bubbling over and without hesitation or permission, Rosa persisted, "Do you think it possible to reconcile *la tradicion hermetica* with feminism? Hoping to do so is what led me to Sor Juana and San Jeronimo, where I have found a spiritual home."

After pausing for several seconds to collect her thoughts regarding the provocative question, Frances ventured, "How commendable, Sor Rosa, you are addressing these significant issue at such a young age, since it is only recently I, a very old woman, have begun to wrestle with them. Indeed, I wonder what's taken me so long...."

"*Gracias, Dama Francesca,*" Rosa flushed, as the Abbess interjected, "Perhaps, Sor Rosa, before we leap into this complicated topic, we should

60

allow Dama Francesca to set forth the tenets of the Hermetic tradition—especially for those of us who are not as immersed in the topic as you are."

"Yes, please, Abadesa," said another of the *monjas* in halting English, "although as best I could I read through Dama Francesca's great book, I regret to say it was challenging for me, so it would help me very much if Dama Francesca herself would talk to us about *la tradicion hermetica*."

"*Por favor*," several other of the nuns murmured.

"*Gracias*, Sor Gertrudis," the Abadesa added, "even though I have read the great book several times, since we are blessed to be in her company, I, too, would like to hear Dama Francesca's personal thoughts regarding how *la tradicion hermetica* has influenced her personal spiritual journey."

Without a doubt this was unlike any of the many academic forums in which Frances had participated during her long career, and collecting her thoughts, she began thoughtfully. Recently she had begun to assemble notes for her autobiography, and as she spoke was aware how unexpected and extraordinary it was to be sharing personal thoughts with a small group of Mexican nuns she had encountered just a few hours ago.

Speaking slowly and deliberately, she began, "*Gracias, Abadesa*, I am honored to bask in the spiritual presence of Sor Juana, and while regrettably I have become acquainted only recently with her remarkable journey and legacy, it is apparent to me she and my protagonist Giordano Bruno share much in common. Since their worldviews encompassed notions of a Universal Church, I identify with both martyrs. My own spiritual yearnings were fostered first by my beloved father, a devout man who advocated what we in England call Anglo-Catholicism—that is to say, the Roman Church before it was shattered in the sixteenth-century by Martin Luther, another maverick priest, who launched what is called the Reformation. This was an effort to reform a church he considered dictatorial and corrupt. Like Bruno, my father yearned for the restoration and harmony of a Universal Church free from doctrinal warfare and bureaucratic tyranny."

"*Claro*," the Abadesa affirmed.

"When people ask me to explain the Hermetic tradition, I usually begin with three words, Mysticism, Gnosticism, and Magic, experiences, which I believe are relevant to all religious traditions. Regardless of our faith—or even if we don't espouse a formal one—at some point each of us has undergone a mystical experience. For example, just now during the Eucharist, I had a sense of being removed, of timelessness."

As Sor Susana translated, the *monjas* nodded their approval while Frances continued, "Simply stated, Gnosticism is self-knowledge, which, as we say in English, is 'easier said than done.' Even though I approach the end of my earthly journey, I regret to say there is a great deal about myself I still do not know and, truth be told, do not always like."

Here the Abadesa interjected, "My dear Dama Francesca, we all share those feelings, and as we acquire maturity and insight, I find they intensify as we age. In fact, isn't that illustrated in the ritual of the Eucharist and why we repeatedly pray for the 'cleansing of our hearts and minds?'"

"Extraordinary," Frances reflected, "here in Mexico in the convent of Sor Juana de la Cruz, I find absolution by one of her disciples."

"What about Magic, Dama Francesca?" ever-ebullient Sor Rosa again interjected. "Isn't magic *supersticioso?*"

"On the contrary, my dear," Frances refuted gently. "In the context of the Hermetic tradition, magic implies spiritual transformation, as exemplified by simple phenomena of nature such as water freezing into ice, an egg becoming hard boiled, or the blossoming of a flower. After all, don't our souls undergo similar changes when we are touched by the Spirit?"

"Of course," the young nun acknowledged.

Concerned she was preaching or sounding too pedantic, Frances paused for a sip of sweet hibiscus tea, but immediately the Abadesa interjected, "Of course, Dama Francesca, this philosophy and history touched Sor Juana's life as well and, I might add, haunts Mexico still today—especially here at San Jeronimo."

Grateful for an opportunity to deflect attention from discomforting personal revelations, which she was not used to sharing publicly, Frances urged, "Please explain, Abadesa, in what way are contentious conflicts of the European Reformation experienced today at San Jeronimo?"

Now she noticed several of the nuns staring down at hands folded into their laps. Had something she said made them uneasy? How she prayed that not be the case! When the Abadesa responded, Frances was both relieved and astonished.

"Dama Francesca, although we have shared our revised ritual with you, I have not been completely candid. By any chance are you familiar with an organization known as the Women's Ordination Conference?"

"Why of course I am!" Frances practically hooted. "Several of my dearest friends and colleagues in London are fervent supporters, and I have been honored to attend several of their monthly meetings. In fact, several months ago I spoke to them regarding remarkable images of an androgynous Christ in the Tarot. Perhaps you too are familiar with the cards. In any event, are you suggesting you and the Sisters of San Jeronimo too are proponents of women priests?"

Visibly breathing a sigh of relief, mirrored by each of her acolytes, the Abadesa smiled broadly, "*Si*, Dama Francesca, secretly we have been affiliated with the conference for the past several years. Needless to say, however, because of the extremely conservative views of the Mexican Antonio Cardinal Mendoza, at all times we must maintain public silence regarding our views. Otherwise we fear the convent will be closed forever and once again the library dispersed—to say nothing of our dwindling order or what would happen to each of us."

Finally, unable to contain herself any longer, the nun who identified herself as Lucia spoke up. "Please, Dama Francesca, tell us about your English compatriots and how they circumvent the grasp of the Vatican."

"Are you a feminist, Dama Francesca?" Sor Rosa once again interjected.

Here was an unexpected turn of events, and caught off guard, Frances, who would have given anything for a Deliciado, once again attempted to collect her wildly ricocheting thoughts.

"Simply stated," she began, "my colleagues in London ignore the Vatican."

"Astounding!" Lucia gasped, "How do they manage that?"

"Well," Frances responded, "while remaining devout Roman Catholics, which they consider their heritage, they are impervious to the threat of excommunication. As you may know, when women's ordinations first began in the 1970s, ex-communication was a given, but these days it is rare for dissidents to be ex-communicated—at least in England, and, I believe, the United States as well. Is that not the case in Mexico?"

At which point, as their shoulders rocked with gentle laughter, several nuns shook their heads.

"And so, like you," Frances continued, "my Catholic friends conduct their own rituals, which is another reason this morning's ceremony was such a remarkably moving experience for me. Yet while I respect and cherish my WOC friends, when it comes to feminism, I must confess I am a latecomer to the cause. Born, as I like to say, at the 'cusp' of the twentieth century and immersed for virtually all my adult life in my pursuit of the Hermetic tradition, the issue never intruded upon my thoughts—until last year, when I was introduced by a feminist colleague to a remarkable book called the *Woman's Encyclopedia of Myths and Secrets* by an American author named Barbara Walker...."

Suddenly the nuns stirred in their chairs and looked surreptitiously at one another. As the saying goes, the silence was deafening, leaving Frances to wonder what she had said and what on earth was happening in the Convent. Soberly and quietly the Abadesa explained, "Indeed, we are familiar with the remarkable encyclopedia, Dama Francesca. Especially in Mexico, where indigenous cultures and the Cult of the Virgen are embedded within Christianity and vital to our national identity, any espousal of matriarchy resonates with many compatriots—especially those of us who revere blessed Sor Juana. Yet Cardinal Mendoza considers the Walker volume so threatening to established patriarchal order it has been banned in religious communities throughout Mexico. Therefore, our only copy, which was brought back from the United States by Sor Susana, when she returned from her studies there, is kept under lock and key in the library and allowed to be withdrawn only with my permission.

Chapter Eighteen

As Frances began her talk, Father Manuel had slipped into the back of the library via a back door and stood undetected in the stacks. For obvious reasons, he had not been invited to the presentation but had been informed by Sor Carmela the noted historian was visiting the Convent and the Cardinal had ordered him to attend surreptitiously.

Both clerics had read *Giordano Bruno and the Hermetic Tradition*. While aware of the (justifiable in their minds) fate of the renegade priest, they feared still in twentieth century Mexico the impact of his message was threatening. To say nothing of its likely appeal to a band of renegade *religiosas*!

As Frances's audience eagerly absorbed her opening remarks regarding the universal and transformational aspects of the Hermetic tradition and how it had enhanced and deepened her faith, Father Manuel fumed and, pointing a finger at her, emerged from the stacks and erupted, "This is blasphemy!"

Gasps and the rustle of habits filled the chamber as all heads turned toward the accuser. Caught completely off guard, momentarily Frances was startled into silence. Virtually apoplectic, the Abadesa realized who had interrupted the long-awaited presentation.

Rising from her chair and looking him in the eye, she pronounced calmly but firmly, "Father Manuel, you were not invited here today and are not welcome in the Convent…"

In heavily accented English, Father Manuel now pointed at her and screeched, "You, a mere *religiosa*, cannot tell me where I belong, Abadesa!"

Immediately upon hearing his angry voice, Sor Carmela had risen from her chair and, turning toward her irate mentor, began to shake her head, which he ignored.

Peering over her glasses, Frances gazed at the red-faced cleric in the back of the library. Far from being intimidated, she was infuriated. Few things exasperated Dame Frances Yates more than being interrupted.

Icily but calmly she queried, "And you, sir, are?"

"I am Father Manuel Gonzales, the Cardinal's lieutenant here in Mexico City, and as an Anglican YOU are a heretic!"

"Certainly, Father Manuel, were he here and in spite of his creed, I am certain the Cardinal, whom admittedly I do not know, would not countenance your bad manners. How dare you point your finger at *me*!" For Frances Yates a pointed finger was like waving a red flag in front of a bull. Then with aplomb and even relish Frances calmly continued, "Father Manuel, long before you were born, I was raised an Anglo-Catholic, taught by true Christians to appreciate and revere the beauty of the once universal Church, as proselytized by Giordano Bruno and the Hermetic tradition to which I have devoted my life's work. It is obdurate bureaucrats like you who have distorted and betrayed the true meaning of Christ's message of tolerance and love. In fact, it is my firm conviction the Vatican's intolerance and quest for raw political power are among the great tragedies in Western civilization, as exemplified by the persecution of Sor Juana de la Cruz in this very convent."

Lost in admiration for Frances's fortitude and verbal dexterity, the Abadesa turned her back on Father Manuel, nodded toward her guest, and with a wry smile took her seat. "My deepest apologies, Dama Francesca— please forgive this very rude intrusion, and if and when you are collected, continue your lecture."

Recognizing he had met his match and been humiliated before a group of *monjas* by an aging British scholar, Father Manuel harrumphed and left the chapel, muttering, "We will see about this..."

"Now, where were we?" Frances smiled at her audience and calmly resumed her talk.

Chapter Nineteen

While Frances visited the convent, Juan Carlos, who had returned to the Majestic to call for them, escorted Elizabeth and Drummond to Chapultepec. After a blissful night tightly spooned against Drummond's strong back, Elizabeth, who loathed hirsute males, sat on the edge of the tub to watch him shave, one of her favorite morning activities.

"Although we'll be with sweet Juan Carlos, don't you think it's nice to have a morning to more or less to ourselves? As much as I revere Dame Frances, I must admit I like having you all to myself for at least a few minutes."

"As do I, my darling," Drummond smiled through a screen of lather, prompting a kiss, which left her cheeks smothered with fragrant shaving cream.

Drummond, who had been widowed and lonely for too long, enjoyed their morning conferences over the sink, and like his new wife, was delighted and surprised to find himself on a Mexican honeymoon. After he splashed his face with the witch hazel after-shave Elizabeth adored and always acknowledged with a cheek-to-cheek rub, the Scotland Yard detective donned his usual uniform of navy blazer, khaki slacks, fresh white shirt, and regimental tie.

Aware it labeled her a "typical" American, when and wherever she travelled, unabashedly Elizabeth tied her prematurely gray hair into a ponytail at the nape of her neck and wore a baseball cap from her sizeable collection. Along with her habitual ensemble of slacks, tailored shirt, a boxy sweater from her equally substantial array and sensible shoes, over her left shoulder she slung a hefty touristy tote with broad comfortable straps she had purchased last year in London. Made in China and stamped with images of famous city monuments, the bag amused Elizabeth because several names, such as "Picadelly" were misspelled. For her trip to Mexico she had chosen a navy cap with an image of the Statue of Liberty on the crown.

As they walked hand in hand to the Terazzo, Elizabeth queried, "Do they have baseball caps in Mexico City? If so, I must have one," which amused her very traditional British husband.

Even though he was on vacation, and despite Juan Carlos's urging in Mexico more casual costume was perfectly acceptable, if not *de rigueur*, Drummond more or less maintained his usual uniform. Although to his mind, navy blazer, khaki slacks with white shirt and tie constituted casual dress, he persisted by maintaining especially in a capital city, it wouldn't feel proper to dress any more casually. Truthfully, it was easier not to have to think about it by changing styles or shoes, and more importantly, jackets provided plenty of pockets for wallets, keys, and other male paraphernalia. Furthermore, he had long been convinced proper attire ensured better treatment in public places and even more significantly he knew maintaining standards was still another reason his lovely new wife appreciated him. Following a leisurely and hearty breakfast, Juan Carlos joined them for coffee and the trip to the grand castle Chapultepec, which dominates the cityscape. Erected in 1785, it is the only royal castle in the Americas, he noted. Even to Drummond, a British citizen, more or less accustomed to royal pomp, it was a remarkable experience. Gazing from the voluptuous aerial garden upon the teeming city beyond, such grandeur seemed incongruous. The more they learned about the tale of the hapless, albeit well-intended European royals who had resided there, their impression was confirmed, and the tragic denouement of their brief sojourn in Mexico seemed a foregone conclusion.

The spacious rooms on the upper floors of the castle were crammed with costly European furniture, artifacts, and regal portraits of the Austrian Emperor and his elegant Belgian Empress. In Maximilian's wood-paneled library, Drummond stopped short before a framed oval lithograph of the emperor in familiar regalia, an apron with an imprinted image, and around his neck a sash from which an inverted triangle was suspended.

Although he was assured of the answer, Drummond asked, "By any chance was Emperor Maximillian a Freemason, Juan Carlos?"

"Honestly, Inspector, I don't know," their usually well-informed tour guide replied. "What makes you think so?"

"It's this image," Drummond indicated. "The emperor is wearing Masonic regalia."

"Are you a Freemason, Inspector?"

"I am," Drummond affirmed. "Do you know of others here in Mexico?"

"I am chagrined to say I do not," Juan Carlos admitted, "although, now that I think about it, I may have seen a portrait of Bolivar in similar costume. Tomorrow when I return to the university I can inquire of my colleagues and look in the library as well."

To mask his chagrin regarding any gap in his knowledge of Mexican history, the aspiring scholar countered, "In the meantime, Inspector, are you aware of Dame Frances's writings regarding the relationship between Freemasonry and the Hermetic tradition—especially as elaborated in her brilliant *Rosicrucian Enlightenment*?"

Not be outdone by the brandishing of an academic—especially one young enough to be his son—and feeling his competitive juices stirring, Drummond, who recently had poured over the book in one night, parried, "Yes, of course, as well as its relationship to the Tarot."

In the midst of his investigation Drummond had benefitted from significant discussions with Frances regarding the roots of Freemasonry. Was he being discourteous toward his host? While he hoped not, immediately Drummond was intrigued with the apparent presence of the Brotherhood here in Mexico.

By the time they toured the elaborate grounds of the castle, any tension had dissipated, and when they reached the patio, Drummond's and Elizabeth's attention was diverted by the story of the *Ninos Heroes* or "Boy Soldiers." In 1847, a mere handful of young Mexican cadets had died defending the castle from invading U. S. forces during the infamous Mexican-American War. Above the staircase Juan Carlos drew their attention to a stunning mural by Gabriel Flores immortalizing one of the young heroes as he soared through the air holding a Mexican flag.

"Indigenous roots coupled with European culture, the tragedy and improbable story of Emperor Maximillian and Empress Carlota, the unjust Mexican-American War, heroic cadets, to say nothing of one of the great revolutions of all time...why don't Americans, and I would guess the British as well, know more about this dramatic and discomforting history, Stuart?"

newly minted historian Elizabeth pondered. Clasping her new husband's strong, firm and always readily available hand, she added. "To say nothing of a tragic love story...."

Drummond shook his head. "Indeed, my dear, the notion of placing an Austrian prince on the throne of Mexico of all places and declaring him emperor strikes me as another example of colonial arrogance at which we British excel. Yet, as we just learned, your own country's Mexican-American War was hardly a noble cause."

"Touché, Stuart, truth be told most of what I know about Mexican history comes from watching Gary Cooper and Burt Lancaster in *Vera Cruz* and *Viva Zapata* with Marlon Brando somewhat incongruously playing Zapata. Do you know either film?"

A film buff, Elizabeth often referred to movies for historical context.

"Isn't it ironic if they learn any history at all, Americans seem to know more about European history than that of their nearest neighbors, most of whom were here long before any of us were? Certainly, the perfidy of the Mexican-American war is glossed over in our history books—*as if* it was justified to grab half of Mexico's territory in the interest of so-called Manifest Destiny! My humble guess, Juan Carlos, is this terrible history looks very different on your side of the border."

"*Claro, Elizabeta*," Juan Carlos acknowledged with no further comment.

"Once again," Elizabeth continued, "I am reminded of the most important lesson I learned in law school, when our illustrious professor Justice Ruth Bader Ginsburg posed in a civil procedure class, 'What is the answer to every question?'"

Having heard the story several times before, Drummond nodded, "It depends!"

"Yes," acknowledging her tendency to repeat herself and grateful for Drummond's patience, Elizabeth smiled, "and as you also know, I believe this lesson applies to the study of history as well. Events always look different to the other side, and what better example than this infamous war that robbed Mexico of half its territory?

"Perhaps when we return to London I'll suggest to Director Hilb readers be offered a class in Latin American history, which I would very much like to teach. After all, Aby Warburg traveled to the American West to learn more about indigenous cultures."

Former attorney turned historian Elizabeth Wolcott-Drummond, as she now introduced herself, had been offered a position as lecturer at the Warburg Institute on Frances's strong recommendation and had readily accepted. With no ties holding her in New York and blissfully at home in London, it was the perfect solution to the challenges of trans-Atlantic logistics unfurled by her unexpected marriage to a Scotland Yard detective. Indeed, in every way it was a dream come true!

Chapter Twenty

When Juan Carlos called for her at three, Frances embraced and thanked Abadesa for a most enthralling and enlightening visit and asked if she might be able to return later in the week to absorb Sor Juana's aura one more time before leaving Mexico.

"There is no need to ask, Dama Francesca," she was assured. "At any and all times you especially will always be welcomed in the Convent. Indeed, we have been blessed by your presence here today."

While elated and stimulated by her revelations in the Convent, Frances was drained and yearned for quiet time to rest and digest the unexpected and extraordinary experience. Still she realized her young companions were looking forward to another enticing dinner. As satisfying as it would be for her, she couldn't expect them to dine again at the Majestic. Truth be told, however, even with the ministrations of Jésus and now that she thought about it, she wouldn't mind another glass or two of sweet sangria! Taking his arm, and in response to his inquiries, Frances effusively thanked Juan Carlos for arranging the extraordinary visit, which, when processed, she was certain would rank among the highlights of her long life.

"I am so very pleased, Dama Francesca," the young Mexican exhaled with relief. "Tonight we must celebrate at another of my favorite bistros, but first and per our custom, may I suggest a refreshing siesta?"

"Gracias, dear Juan Carlos," Frances sighed with relief, "once again you have read my mind!"

Chapter Twenty-One

At the historic Hosteria Santo Domingo, Drummond slipped his credit card to the captain who seated them. While Frances's travel and entertainment expenses were covered by the Warburg, tonight's party was his treat. Settled at a quiet corner table toward the back of the bistro, the four colleagues sipped sangria and munched on multi-colored corn chips with guacamole.

Elizabeth launched the discussion, "Please tell us, Dame Frances, about your visit to the Convent."

"It was enthralling, but first things first," Frances countered. "Please tell us about this marvelous restaurant, Juan Carlos, and then, Elizabeth, onto Chapultepec. To tell the truth, I am still processing the extraordinary experience, which I must admit has quite overwhelmed me, so if you'll indulge me, I find I need a bit more time to organize my thoughts before expressing them."

"Of course, forgive me, Dame Frances," Elizabeth complied immediately and turned to Juan Carlos, "You first, Juan Carlos..."

Gesturing toward the ornate high ceiling, Juan Carlos informed them they were in the former Dominican convent of Santo Domingo and the Hosteria, established in 1860, is the oldest restaurant in Mexico City.

"Furthermore," he continued, "it is renowned as the 'Cathedral of *chiles en nogado*,' a famous dish, which I've ordered ahead of time and insist you try. Legend has it the recipe was created in the 1820s in the city of Puebla by the nuns of Santa Monica to honor our great General Iturbide."

When a steaming platter arrived at the table, the visitors immediately understood its significance. Green chilies were topped with a creamy white sauce Juan Carlos informed them was "*nogado*" (walnut), along with red pomegranate seeds, the colors of the Mexican flag.

As she lifted her laden fork, Elizabeth noted with anticipation, "The subject of food and history has always interested me—perhaps, Dame Frances, it could be a topic for a seminar at the Warburg."

"Capital idea, Elizabeth!" Frances agreed, as she too ventured into culinary history and breathed a sigh of relief the exotic flavors weren't overly spicy; in fact, it was delicious. "Now please tell me about your visit to Chapultepec."

"If not quite as profound experience as yours, I too found our visit to the castle revelatory," Elizabeth responded. "First and foremost for me was the awareness how little we in the United States know about Mexican history, which is still another topic I would like to explore in my reading and writing, as well as teaching."

"I, too, feel my worldview has been expanded dramatically after just three days in Mexico," at last Frances ventured, as her young colleagues listened attentively. "Yesterday at Guadalupe and today in the Convent, where much to my astonishment I discovered the nuns are advocates of the Women's Ordination Conference. Today they celebrated the Eucharist without a priest being present. Dare I say it was not at all difficult for me to image Sor Juana herself presiding?"

Then relating the story of Father Manuel's intrusion on her talk to her astounded companions, Frances inquired, "Although hoping not to discomfort you, Juan Carlos, I wonder if you are aware of this situation."

"I am not, Dama Francesca," he responded soberly, "and of course I apologize and deeply regret it occurred."

"Then, perhaps my friends, in light of possible serious consequences for the residents of the Convent, we should keep this intelligence among ourselves," Frances counseled. The meal ended in a subdued mood with a shared dessert of sweet potato with pineapple and a plate of snowy white Mexican wedding cookies.

Chapter Twenty-Two

On the walk back to the Majestic Elizabeth asked, "What have you planned for us tomorrow, Juan Carlos?"

"Tomorrow I suggest a visit to the neighborhood of Coyoacan and Casa Azul, the home of Frida Kahlo."

"Marvelous," pronounced Elizabeth, who couldn't wait to see the setting of the riveting movie "Frida" that had thrilled her and earned so many awards.

But on Thursday morning, along with the usual morning trumpet blasts, Frances was jolted awake by a very early phone call from Inspector Drummond.

"Forgive me for calling so early, Dame Frances, but I'm afraid I have distressing news. A few minutes ago, Juan Carlos, not wanting to upset you so early, called to inform me there has been an unfortunate and disturbing incident in the convent.

"Good Lord, Inspector, what on earth has happened? I hope no one has been harmed," Frances virtually barked into the phone.

"Unfortunately and from what I understand," Drummond responded, "it seems one of the nuns has been found dead on the floor of the library. I am sorry to report further there is the possibility of foul play."

"Not again," Frances moaned, as a vision of the dead body of a former archivist in the stacks of the Warburg Institute flashed vividly through her mind.

"Do you know who it is?"

To her chagrin, Frances prayed the dead nun wasn't radiant, young Sor Rosa and consequently breathed a sigh of relief when Drummond responded soberly, "I believe the name Juan Carlos relayed was Sor Angela. Do you know her?"

"Yes," Frances replied, "Sor Angela played the guitar while we sang hymns during the service."

Drummond continued, "It seems, when informed by Juan Carlos that I am affiliated with Scotland Yard, the Mexican authorities have requested I might serve as a consultant to the investigation. Furthermore, given your recent encounter with the nuns, which potentially can provide additional insight regarding the community, I suggested you too be invited to the meeting, and of course, I would like, and have requested, Elizabeth share her legal expertise as well."

"Of course, Inspector, although honestly, even after spending several hours with them I'm afraid I can't recall all of the nuns' names and faces. Dressed alike in their habits, it was difficult to keep them straight," Frances remarked. "Truly, this is horrific news! Give me a few minutes to dress, and I will meet you and Elizabeth in the lobby."

Somehow, she managed to assemble some clothes, haphazardly run a brush through her tangled hair, and hurry toward the elevator. As she waited for it to arrive, Frances realized, in fact, she did remember young, charming Sor Rosa, along with Sor Susana, who translated for the discussion, and dour librarian Sor Carmela.

Chapter Twenty-Three

With Elizabeth and Drummond at each of Frances' elbows, the three colleagues walked as quickly as they could across the Zócalo. Arriving at the convent, it was unsettling and seemingly incongruous to find two police cars with flashing red lights parked at the entrance. When Drummond presented his identification and introduced Frances and Elizabeth to the uniformed officer standing guard, it appeared they were expected. Immediately another officer escorted them to the library. There they found Juan Carlos, along with a somber cast of characters, dressed in various uniforms and religious habits, gathered around what appeared to be a body on the floor, covered by a dark blanket. Several of the nuns were crying and with tears in her eyes, the Abadesa approached Frances. Instinctively both women held out their hands to greet and console one another.

"Oh, Dama Francesca, I am so sorry to have to share this tragedy with you and your friends. What a horrible introduction to Sor Juana's blessed sanctuary!"

"I too mourn, Abadesa, especially whenever temples of enlightenment and learning are defiled with violence and death. Unfortunately, recently my own and beloved Warburg Institute experienced a similar disturbing incident. Since my colleagues Inspector Drummond and Dr. Wolcott shared those unhappy times, I am comforted by their presence here."

"*De nuevo,* Inspector and Doctora Wolcott," murmured the Abadesa, while extending several delicate limp fingers to Frances's companions. "In turn, may I introduce Inspector Pedro Guzman of the PFM, Bureau of Ministerial Policia."

Although not quite as tall, like Drummond, Pedro Guzman exuded authority and competence. Wearing a well-tailored dark suit and white shirt with a striped tie, his dark eyes were intense, and his trimmed, dark hair was slicked back from a notable forehead.

With commanding demeanor, the Mexican official firmly and confidently shook Drummond's hand. "It is an honor to meet a representative from Scotland Yard," Guzman said in slightly accented and impeccable English. "Any insights you may have regarding this unfortunate death are appreciated."

"Understood," Drummond nodded solemnly. Then to his astonishment he noticed the Mexican Inspector was wearing a remarkable lapel pin. There could be little doubt regarding the significance of a square and compass. "Are you a traveler, Inspector?"

"*Si*," Guzman's eyes lit up, as he replied with a slight smile and curt nod, "I am traveling east!"

Along with an exotic honeymoon, little did Inspector Stuart Drummond expect to encounter a fellow Freemason in Mexico! As he and Guzman acknowledged one another, they placed their thumbs over each other's second knuckles and firmly exchanged a surreptitious handshake.

Now Guzman introduced the fourth man in the room: Father Manuel Gonzales, a delegate from the Congregation for the Propagation of the Faith, who represented Mexican Cardinal Felipé Mendoza. Cardinal Mendoza, they were informed was the longtime presiding Catholic official overseeing all of Mexico. With a slight paunch and close-cropped white hair, Gonzales was a small, stocky man in his fifties. Exacerbated by a clerical collar and long black cassock, his scowling demeanor exemplified to Elizbeth the stereotype of an unforgiving priest.

According to Guzman, who shared the insight *sotto voce* with Drummond, Mendoza was archly conservative, and among Catholic circles it was generally known there was no love lost between the Cardinal and the feisty inhabitants of San Geronimo.

Both Frances and Elizabeth noted the only dry-eyed nun was Sor Carmela, who once again appeared to be anxious and impatient. With decades of experience at the Warburg and at libraries across Europe, Frances knew full well librarians could be abrupt, autocratic, possessive and downright crotchety. Occasionally she even wondered if, along with cataloging, some of them took courses in gruff behavior. *In all likelihood,* Frances presumed, *she resents intruders in her library.*

Chapter Twenty-Four

Impatient with Drummond's and Guzman's murmured exchanges and curious as ever, Frances approached and leaned over the wrapped body. Stunned by her recklessness, both police inspectors watched as—without taking into account any forensic consequences—Frances leaned over and unfolded the blanket covering it. Seeing Sor Angela was clutching a thick, black book, she reached down and turned it over.

Too late, but with as much politesse as he could muster under the circumstances, Guzman reprimanded Frances, "*Por favor*, Dama Francesca, it is best not to tamper with evidence. May I please have the book?"

But as if thunderstruck and completely ignoring his admonition, Frances stared at the book she now held. Immediately she had recognized the cover of a worn paperback copy of Barbara Walker's *Woman's Encyclopedia of Myths and Secrets*. Here was the very book that had transformed her views regarding feminism and feminist theology. Why was the deceased nun clutching it? Could somehow a book have something to do with Sor Angela's untimely death?

Chapter Twenty-Five

Whereupon and although of course he too knew better, Inspector Drummond leaned over the body and carefully lifted Sor Angela's coif. "Furthermore, look here, Inspector Guzman, there are bruises on Sor Angela's neck. With the broken glasses as added evidence, I'm sorry to say it appears this death may not be an accident!"

To everyone's further astonishment, Father Manuel, who had been quietly observing the scene, turned scarlet and erupted in furious Spanish, "Abadesa, what is that filthy book still doing in the convent? As you have been informed, the Cardinal has banned this infamy from all diocese libraries!"

"What is he saying?" Frances and Elizabeth whispered simultaneously to Juan Carlos.

"It seems the book has upset him," Juan Carlos responded, while trying to follow the unfolding drama.

Whirling abruptly and pointing at Frances, Father Manuel continued his rant, "Furthermore, what is this foreigner and champion of the heretic Bruno doing in the Convent? At least the Church knew what to do with *him*!"

Neither Frances nor anyone else had to speak Spanish to understand the gist of what the crazed priest was saying. Witnessing his rage, they all had heard "Bruno…"

Blindsided once again, Frances sat down on the nearest wooden chair while Elizabeth reached for her hand, and white as a ghost, Juan Carlos knelt at her side murmuring soothing words of comfort and apology.

Without a moment's hesitation, once again the Abadesa ferociously denounced the erratic priest who continued to glare at Frances and still quivered with rage. "Father Manuel, your comportment is unacceptable! In the face of death in this holy place and in the name of Sor Juana de la Cruz, I demand you immediately desist and apologize at once to Dama Francesca!"

Yet there seemed no way to corral the arrogant priest's fury, which he now turned on the Abadesa as well.

"How dare *you*, a mere woman and renegade nun, chastise *me*! Along with the blasphemies perpetuated in the Convent, which are known to him and the Vatican as well, the Cardinal will hear about this incident at once."

"He most certainly will," the Abadesa asserted calmly and confidently. "Your desecration of this sacred place and rudeness to an esteemed scholar are not only unacceptable but intolerant, un-Christian, and bring shame upon us all!"

"We'll see about that," Father Manuel screeched, as, nearly knocking her off balance, he brushed the Abadesa aside and moved toward the doorway.

Quickly taking charge of the chaos, Inspector Guzman stood in his path. "One moment, Father, before you leave, I would like a few words with you," and grasping the trembling cleric by the elbow, he escorted him to the hallway outside the library.

"While your rude behavior embarrasses us all and brings shame to all Mexico, at 9:00 A.M. tomorrow morning you are ordered to return here in better humor to discuss the death of Sor Angela. If you are not here at nine sharp, along with officers and handcuffs, I personally will come to the palace to escort you and bring you here for questioning. In the meantime, if you or the Cardinal have any questions regarding these instructions—or my jurisdiction—you may contact my supervisor at police headquarters. Is that understood?"

Without a word, the furious cleric glared at Guzman and marched past the policemen, down the stone stairway, and out the door of the convent.

Chapter Twenty-Six

When Guzman, irate and chagrined, returned to the library, he was surprised to see Frances and the other witnesses to the stunning scene engaged in animated conversation. Still seated and surrounded by her solicitous colleagues and far from cowed, Dame Frances appeared to be holding court.

"*Mis amigos*," Guzman interjected, "I so regret this dreadful incident and on behalf of my country apologize sincerely."

"There is no need for you to apologize, Inspector. I am quite recovered from what admittedly was an unexpected assault," Frances immediately assured him. "Yet what astounds me is, even in the face of death and centuries later, the priority of the Church appears still to be blatant hostility to any perceived intrusion on patriarchal dictum. Although Giordano Bruno was martyred in Rome several centuries ago, the power of his message of universality seems as threatening as ever, even in twentieth-century Mexico."

"To say nothing of women's voices!" Elizabeth added, "The *Woman's Encyclopedia* seems especially to infuriate him."

Meanwhile, kneeling beside the body of her dead librarian, the Abadesa mouthed a silent prayer while Juan Carlos stood nearby, crossed himself, and bowed his head.

Chapter Twenty-Seven

Sensing Guzman's dismay and distraction and ever the consummate professional, Drummond now made an effort to help refocus attention on the death in the convent.

"Inspector, in light of Father Manuel's irrational reaction, it occurs to me the incident may be more complex than might appear. In similar situations it has been my experience frequently first impressions are too simplistic."

Nodding his head, Guzman responded, "*Claro*, Inspector, what are your initial thoughts?"

Surprisingly, it was Frances who interceded. "If I may, Inspector, in light of obvious tensions in the convent, perhaps Sor Angela wasn't attempting to read the encyclopedia. Instead, it occurs to me, she may have been trying to protect the volume from someone who was offended it was here and may have been trying to remove it from the library. What if inadvertently she discovered someone else in the process of trying to take the book and, to prevent that from happening, managed to wrestle it from the culprit? After all, don't her broken and twisted glasses suggest a struggle of some kind?"

"Brava, Dame Frances!" both detectives and Elizabeth declared simultaneously.

"What's more," Frances continued, as with fleshy arms crossed over her generous bosom and her glasses, attached to a black ribbon, perched on her fleshy nose, she sat resolutely observing the scene, "it seems to me *if* Sor Angela herself were trying to steal the book, the person who tried to stop her would have reported the unfortunate incident to the Abadesa immediately—especially if it were one of the other nuns. Therefore, it occurs to me someone from outside the convent may have attempted to remove the encyclopedia from the library."

"Still another perceptive suggestion, Dame Frances," Drummond condurred, "and unless there are signs of a forcible break in, we could rule out an unknown intruder."

"And/or," Elizabeth added, "could an outside visitor have had an accomplice inside the convent?"

"What are you suggesting, Doctora?" Guzman inquired.

"Well, it seems to me," Elizabeth noted, "any outsider intending to remove a specific book from the library in the middle of the night would have to know precisely where to find it, or to guarantee a speedy departure have it readily available when he or she arrived, and if that is the case, then the plan might have been to have someone waiting for him with the book in hand."

With a slight smile and nod of approval toward his wife, Drummond quickly followed her lead. "This makes sense, Elizabeth, and if it is in fact the case, it seems to me it narrows the list of suspects to consider...."

"Well done, my dear," Frances added, patting Elizabeth's hand approvingly.

"What fine detectives and collaborators you are!" Guzman exclaimed. "Just now I have ordered Father Manuel to return to the convent tomorrow morning for questioning, and with your cooperation, Abadesa, this afternoon I would like to arrange to meet with you and the other *monjas* as well. Presumably none of you will leave the convent in the meantime. And while of course I appreciate your position, for the sake of the integrity of the official investigation, I prefer to interview the *monjas* individually without your supervision."

Then catching them off guard, Guzman startled Drummond and Elizabeth with a request that they participate in the interviews. "The esteemed professionalism of Scotland Yard would be appreciated as well, Inspector Drummond, and the presence of an experienced *abogada* also would be helpful, Doctora Wolcott, as well, I believe, reassuring to the *religiosas*. Frankly, I would like an impartial woman to be present when I speak with them."

Exchanging glances and nodding curtly to one another, Elizabeth and Drummond immediately agreed.

"Of course we also will look into the possible presence of any workmen or delivery people, although what any of them would be doing in the library in the middle of the night is doubtful," Guzman noted in a take-charge manner Drummond appreciated and admired.

Turning to one of his associates standing at the doorway, Guzman informed them, "This is Sargento Torres from my office who, when needed, will serve as our translator."

"Very well," the Abadesa rose stiffly from her chair, "since I am no longer needed here, I will begin to arrange the interviews for tomorrow."

In an obvious huff the regal Abadesa swept from the room, trailed by several weepy nuns and Sor Carmela, who, Elizabeth had noticed, had been standing aloof and sullen behind the desk.

"Finally, please forgive me, Dama Francesca," Guzman bowed toward Frances, "but most respectfully and despite your brilliant observations this morning, in light of the unforgiveable outburst of Father Manuel, I do not think it prudent for you as well to participate in the interrogations. Therefore, I suggest you *not* join us tomorrow for the interviews. However, since I have invited them to join me, I urge Inspector Drummond and Doctora Wolcott to keep you apprised of our progress. In this way you can monitor the investigation, and in the event you have any further insights, I urge you to share them with us."

Concerned about Frances's feelings and far from insignificant ego, Elizabeth and Drummond held their breath, but Frances surprised them both with a quick nod of her leonine head.

"Agreed, Inspector, thank you for your consideration."

In fact, Frances was enormously relieved to escape the ugly scene. Although at first stunned by Father Manuel's attack, quickly she now realized she was consumed with anger: anger at the unnecessary death of an innocent young woman; anger at the calcified Church establishment, as personified by the belligerent priest; and anger, once again, her own spiritual tranquility had been disturbed by violence. As she made her way out of the defiled library, dreadful thoughts of the recent similar incident in her beloved Warburg flashed through her mind.

Nodding to Elizabeth and Drummond and leaning on the strong arm of Juan Carlos, who had been overlooked in the tumult, Frances was enormously relieved to be able to flee the scene of the crime.

Before the visitors departed, Inspector Guzman took Drummond aside. "If I may, Inspector, as it happens tomorrow evening is the monthly meeting of the Lautero Lodge here in Mexico City, and while I regret the unhappy circumstances of our encounter, I wonder if you would care to accompany me to the meeting. Perhaps your young friend Juan Carlos could join us as well."

"It would be an honor, Inspector," Drummond affirmed, exchanging another ritual handshake with his newfound Mexican colleague.

Chapter Twenty-Eight

Father Manuel Gonzales couldn't remember a day in his life when he wasn't furious about something. His own mother had once observed she thought he was born angry. In all likelihood this had something to do with his missing father, who had disappeared before Manuel was born. Certainly, Mariana Gonzales was overwhelmed with bitterness when she found herself unmarried and left alone at sixteen in the small mountain town of Puebla with a screeching baby. Manuel couldn't remember her ever smiling. To say the least, tender, loving care of an unwanted infant was not her strong suit, and he never experienced a hug or encouraging word.

But for the priests and nuns at the cathedral, he often wondered what would have happened to him and his mother. Finding thankless employment as a cleaning lady at the cathedral enabled Mariana to feed them and to enroll Manuel in the parochial school, where soon it became apparent the unwanted *muchacho* was very bright. Finally, someone seemed to notice and care for him. Early on, young Manuel became the protégé of Father Enrique Mendoza, who taught Latin and the Catechism. The priests who taught at the school for underprivileged boys were unquestioning orthodox Dominicans, very strict, and not adverse to corporal punishment. Without question the conservative Catholic interpretation of the Scriptures and rigid adherence to traditional liturgy incorporated patriarchal views of Eve's sinfulness that tainted all women. Excluding a few caring nuns he encountered along the way, Manuel had never met a single woman he admired—except of course the Blessed Guadalupe.

Over the years, Father Enrique, a talented administrator and perceptive politician, steadily rose in the Catholic hierarchy to become Archbishop of Mexico City. At the same time, he shepherded Manuel through seminary. By the time Manuel completed his studies and became a novice priest, he had earned a reputation as a hothead. Devoted to his mentor, Father Manuel became Father Enrique's trusted assistant and surrogate and seldom left his side. When he did, it was only to carry out Enrique's orders without question.

Upon being named archbishop of the teeming diocese, one of the issues with which the new prelate wrestled was what to do about the feisty *monjas* at the Convent of San Jeronimo. Once renowned but now sparsely populated, the convent had been left largely ignored by his predecessors. Longtime Abadesa Teresa created few waves, and the convent's finances appeared in good order, but recently, along with reports of bizarre rituals being performed in the convent, an anonymous source had conveyed via Father Manuel news of interest in the heretical Women's Ordination Conference or WOC, which advocated women priests. The possibility the Catholic Church might one day follow the lead of the Anglicans, who began to ordain women in the 1970s, was intolerable.

The Archbishop sent his trusted lieutenant to investigate, and Father Manuel began his weekly visits to San Jeronimo. On one recent visit to the library, librarian Sor Carmela had shown Father Manuel a copy of the *Woman's Encyclopedia of Myths and Secrets,* which had recently been added to the renowned collection. As he sat at a long table examining the illustrated volume, and even though his English was somewhat limited, Father Garcia thought his brain would explode. Outrageous notions of a Great Mother and an original Trinity composed of Mother, Daughter, and Holy Crone or "grandmother," as represented in the Christian tradition by St. Anne, mother of the Virgin Mary, were just a few of the blasphemies he encountered.

Chapter Twenty-Nine

Soon after she was named convent librarian, Sor Carmela and Father Manuel realized they had something in common. During his weekly visits to the library, their mutual disdain for the Abadesa became apparent. Exchanging observations and anecdotes, the angry priest and resentful nun forged a bond. In the opinion of Father Manuel, the Abadesa was both haughty and disobedient, frequently choosing to ignore directives from the diocese.

"The woman doesn't know her place!" Father Manuel seethed after each difficult meeting. To Sor Carmela, Teresa was standing in the way of her ambition to succeed her as head of the Convent. Perhaps they could further one another's goals by sewing discord and undermining the Abadesa's regime. Fed by Carmela's reports, Father Manuel questioned every Convent expenditure, including for foodstuffs not grown in the garden, office supplies, earnings from produce sales at a booth in the Zócalo, and small allowances for the *monjas* to purchase personal necessities.

The library was a special target for Father Manuel. At the same time, the Abadesa was determined to reestablish, preserve, and enhance Sor Juana's collection. It seemed opposing goals regarding the convent library had become a shared obsession. Each new volume added to the collection was examined and evaluated by the duo before being catalogued and placed on the shelves. Some never were and instead disappeared into Father Manuel's briefcase then carried out of the Convent. Never a sycophant of Sor Juana, Father Manuel thought the Abadesa's goal frivolous. To Carmela it meant nothing more than extra work. If it weren't for straight-laced, efficient, and worldly Sor Susana, the valuable collection would have fallen into chaos and neglect.

The arrival in the library of the *Woman's Encyclopedia of Myths and Secrets*, followed soon thereafter by hints of the infiltration among the community of the goals of the Women's Ordination Conference, cemented the alliance of the malcontents. When the Abadesa dared to conduct the Eucharist herself and Carmela relayed the news to Father Manuel, it was the last straw. As she reported to him, Carmela refused to take part in the blasphemous feminist celebrations.

"*Madre de Dios!* The Cardinal will hear about this, Sor Carmela," Father Manuel seethed. "And I am certain he will be pleased with your faithfulness, but until I speak with him, and in order not to arouse suspicions, since as we know the walls have ears, I think the encyclopedia should remain under lock and key in the Convent."

Chapter Thirty

After his abrupt dismissal from the Convent of San Geronimo by Inspector Guzman and the order to return the next morning, Father Manuel virtually boiled over with rage.

"How dare that minor bureaucrat! Doesn't he know who I am or for whom I work?" Manuel cursed aloud, crashing into strolling tourists and shoppers as he made his way ferociously back to the Archbishop's headquarters. "Once and for all, the blasphemous feminism of the Abadesa has gone too far and at long last must be put to a stop! To say nothing of that overrated, overweight, and haughty English hag, a misguided Anglican and champion of the heretic Bruno no less. Truly I regret we no longer are allowed to burn them all in the Zocolo!"

By the time Manuel reached the Cathedral, he was covered with sweat and purple with anger. Still he knew he must calm down and collect himself before reporting to the Archbishop, but how to explain disastrous developments in the convent....

As if from central casting, Cardinal Enrique Mendoza personified the Inquisition. Tall and imposing with strong mestizo features, a deep, booming voice and a volatile temper, he played his part well, officiating impeccably over seasonal rituals at the Cathedral. Fearful of becoming targets of his rage, staff and clerical subordinates acceded obsequiously to every order. Far from ever being considered liberal, over the years and in the face of an increasingly secular Mexico, the Cardinal had become even more ferociously conservative, yet nothing had ever ignited his rage more than Father Manuel's reports regarding the infiltration of the Women's Ordination Conference in the Convent.

No one was more familiar with the Cardinal's proclivities than Manuel Gonzales, who had known him since his early childhood and owed everything he had achieved to his mentor, the father he had never had. Although the Cardinal was far from affectionate or loving, Father Manuel never lost sight of the likelihood, but for his guidance and generosity, Manuel Gonzales at most would have become a semi-literate day laborer. As the Cardinal rose through the Church hierarchy, Father Manuel stood unfailingly by his side and now was regarded in Catholic bureaucracy throughout Mexico City as a voice of authority—not to mention how much he appreciated a refined lifestyle of elegant surroundings with good food, fine wine, and trained servants.

Meeting in the Cardinal's elegant Cathedral office with deep red walls, velvet draperies flowered with lush pomegranates, thick Oriental carpets, and centuries old murals of religious scenes on the walls, his protégé revealed recent startling developments in the Convent.

"What are you saying, Manuel?" the Cardinal bellowed when Manuel first reported Abadesa Teresa was presiding over the Eucharist in the chapel. "A woman dared to touch the Elements? Impossible! Outrageous! Do all of the *monjas* participate? Who told you this?"

"The librarian Sor Carmela has become a trusted ally, Your Eminence," Gonzales informed his patron. "While refusing to participate herself, she has witnessed the ceremony, shared eagerly by the other *monjas*. Further, she has informed me a new book has been added to Sor Juana's collection." Relishing and stoking the Cardinal's simmering rage, a skill he had perfected over the years, Father Manuel continued, "It is by an American and called *The Woman's Encyclopedia of Myths and Secrets*. Yesterday I examined the blatantly feminist heresy, and among its outrageous tenets is the notion the original Trinity was composed of Mother, Daughter, and Holy Crone, which the author proclaims was appropriated by Christianity. Accordingly, the Abadesa and *monjas* offer prayers and petitions in the name of a so-called Great Mother."

Leaping from his seat, which resembled a throne, the red-faced Cardinal shouted, "How did this happen? Who introduced such a book to Mexico?"

"It seems the half-American, Sor Susana, who assists Sor Carmela in the library, brought the book back with her when she returned from her studies in the United States, and the Abadesa determined it a worthwhile addition to the Convent's collection."

"Witches!" The Cardinal pounded the massive carved desk then decreed, "The heretical book must be removed immediately from the Convent!"

Chapter Thirty-One

Acutely aware they had been dismissed from the proceedings, Juan Carlos steered Frances down the steep, stone stairway and out of the convent to the courtyard, whereupon she virtually moaned, "Thank you, dear Juan Carlos, really I must have a cigarette! Do you think we might stop on the way back to the Majestic for some refreshment?"

"Of course, Dama Francesca, I know just the spot for a *merienda*, what you call a snack."

Just off the Zócalo, the café Cielto Querido was *intime* and quiet. Tiny blue and red tiles covered the floor and walls and beyond the counter were two cushioned club chairs beside a little round, red metal table. Large, open windows provided a fresh breeze, along with the genial buzz of the square. As she sank into a commodious chair, Frances was relieved to see a small, glass ashtray with a bright blue book of matches imprinted "Cielito Querido" on the table.

"Thank goodness, Mexico City has not totally succumbed to oppressive smoking correctness," she commented, as she retrieved a Deliciado from her battered leather sack. Sighing, she exhaled after stowing the imprinted matches as a souvenir. "Along with convents, I thought libraries were supposed to be hallowed places...."

"It has been a horrific experience, Dama Francesca! Truly I am mortified for my country and so regret involving you in this terrible business. Who could imagine, as you have suggested, the tragic death of valiant Sor Angela, may have been the result of her attempt to safeguard ancient and sacred knowledge?"

"In no way, my dear, is this contretemps your fault," Frances assuaged her former pupil, "but for your generous invitation and hospitality, I never would have encountered Sor Juana and her relationship to the Hermetic tradition. To say nothing of the delights of your vibrant country and those delicious margaritas!"

Laughing out loud and breathing a sigh of relief, Juan Carlos reached across the small table for her wrinkled hand and murmured, "*Muchas gracias, querida Profesora....*"

"Yet how is it possible in this day and age the written word still can arouse such fear and hatred, and what, I wonder, is the *real* issue in the Convent?" Frances pondered. "But before we take it upon ourselves to consider such weighty matters, Juan Carlos, would it be frivolous of me to request a spot of tea? Somehow, along with a Woodbine—or now I should say Deliciado—it always helps to clear my head and calm my nerves."

"Of course, Dama Francesca," Juan Carlos jumped to his feet, "how thoughtless of me! And perhaps something sweet to accompany it...."

"That would be lovely," Frances nodded with an eager smile, "perhaps, if possible, some kind of custard?"

Within minutes the gallant, young Mexican returned from the counter with round, red metal tray bearing two cups, coffee for him and a steaming silver pot of fragrant chamomile tea for Frances, two heavy, round, white china plates with forks, and on each, giant wedges of chocolate custard cake topped with a mound of sweet whipped cream and a giant fresh strawberry.

As he handed her a fresh, colorful, flowered cotton napkin and the sweet cream slid over her tongue, leaving a dark dollop the size of a raisin on her chin, Frances sighed, "Divine!" Then somewhat coyly in her few words of British accented Spanish, she added, "*Gracias, mi amigo!*"

"*Un placer, Profesora.*"

"Tell me about your family, Juan Carlos," Frances inquired. "Just this morning, I am chagrined to admit, I realized, in spite of the time we have spent together here and in London, I know very little about you. How did you discover Bruno, and what took you to the Warburg Institute?"

With his customary gracious smile, Juan Carlos gently placed his hand over Frances's wrinkled fingers. "Thank you for asking, Dama Francesca.

Along with my parents, it is Giordano Bruno and you who led me to the Warburg. Perhaps you will find my family's story of interest. My mother, Carlota, is a former nun, and my father, Juan, was once a priest. They fell in love and married thirty-five years ago. Of course, they were immediately excommunicated. Today they still live in Cuernavaca, where I was born. An only child, I am named for both of them. How I wish you could meet one another! Perhaps we can arrange a visit on your next trip to Mexico."

"At my age, my dear young friend," Frances quipped, "a most unlikely possibility! Tell me about them instead."

"From a traditional Catholic family, my mother was a novice at the Convent of Tepoztlan in Cuernavaca. As you know, in observant families it is considered a mark of achievement if at least one member becomes a *monja* or *cura*. My father was a young priest in training at the magnificent Catedral de la Asuncion in Cuernavaca, assigned to hear the confessions of the young novitiates in the convent.

"When he first heard my mother's sweet voice, my father was enchanted. 'What possible sin could this young innocent have committed?' he wondered. Of course they were minimal, having to do with critical thoughts regarding her lack of dedication to her studies or the food in the convent, but as their weekly visits continued and she felt more comfortable with the kind voice on the other side of the screen, Sor Carlota confessed to more indiscretions.

"It seems she questioned the doctrine of Original Sin, as well as the role of women, as decreed by the Church. Were infants really born laden with sin, and were she and the other novitiates wicked just because they were women?

"At first my father, who came from a family of clerics, was conflicted as well as challenged. In fact, he had begun to question a life of celibacy. At a loss for an adequate response to her provocative questions, he simply advised Carlota to pray longer and harder, but one week, when he hoped she would return to confess more sinful thoughts, violating protocol, he peered through the curtain as she approached the confessional...and fell in love!"

So thoroughly engaged in the tale that she left her Delicioso smoldering in the ashtray, Frances leaned forward and urged, "Please go on...."

"Well, as you English say, to make a long story short, my parents continued to meet in the confessional and, yearning to be together forever, plotted an escape. One night several weeks later, Carlota slipped away from the convent and met my father in the garden, where, wrapped in each other's arms, they spent the night. Early the next morning they were married by a justice of the peace in Cuernavaca.

"But how and where to live? Fortunately, one of my mother's sympathetic sisters took them in. Eventually, my father found employment as a librarian in the Museo Robert Brady, while my mother, who soon found herself pregnant, helped her sister care for her children. Along with the American Peggy Guggenheim, Brady was an ex-pat who had settled in Cuernavaca and created a substantial library and notable art collection.

"In the afternoons, while their babies napped, my mother and her sister read aloud the poetry of Sor Juana de la Cruz, which Carlota had studied in the convent. Meanwhile, among the volumes in Brady's library, my father discovered a copy of your *Bruno and the Hermetic Tradition*. Since both my parents continued to seek spiritual enlightenment and solace, these books were quite literally an answer to prayer. Thus, raised in the company of Sor Juana and Giordano Bruno, who eventually led me to the Convent of San Jeronimo and from there to you in London, whenever someone asks whether I am a Catholic, I reply, 'No, I am a Hermetic!'"

By now Frances was in tears. "Profound thanks for sharing this remarkable and beautiful story, my dear, young friend. Whatever the paths you and your family have followed, miraculously—or one might even say, providentially—it seems they have brought us together, and I am so very grateful you have graced my life. Now where were we?" Wiping her tears with her napkin, she collected herself, "Ah, yes...how tragic and ironic here and now more than a half century later, Mexico and Central America seem still to be in the maw of reactionary Roman Catholicism."

"Of course, not all of us adhere to that line of thinking, Dama Francesca," Juan Carlos responded defensively. "In fact, overall I'd say the patriarchal Roman Church lost its iron grip on Mexico with the Revolution in the first decades of the twentieth century. In any event, as illustrated by the legend of la Virgen de Guadalupe, Mexico's interpretation of the Christian message has always been uniquely feminist."

"Point well taken," Frances acceded, as she ingested another morsel of the heavenly, thick, dark custard, this time wiping her chin with the tear-stained napkin. Then pausing to gaze into space, she pondered. "Yet looking at it another way, one could imagine this extraordinary ongoing reverence for a female goddess, which of course the Virgin Mother represents, is precisely what is so troubling to Father Manuel and his superiors."

"...which could explain his hostility toward the encyclopedia," Juan Carlos astutely followed her lead. "You don't suppose the real issue in the Convent is, still in this day and age, Father Manuel and his cohorts are fearful of the spirit of Sor Juana de la Cruz?"

Chapter Thirty-Two

"Dama Francesca, I have an idea. Since we have been recused from the interrogations, do you think it would be inappropriate if perhaps tomorrow and the next day, while unfortunately our friends remain entangled in the terrible events in the Convent, we did some exploring?"

Seeing her eyes light up and sensing an opening, Juan Carlos persevered, "It occurs to me two particular sites, including the one I had planned for today, would be of particular interest to you. At the same time, I hope and pray they might also serve to distance us somewhat from current woes and instead focus our minds upon loftier thoughts."

Naturally this appeal to both her intellect and spirit aroused Frances's curiosity, while serving to relieve the angst created by the morning's events. As she simultaneously quashed her Deliciado and savored the last bite of dark custard, she felt her ever-vibrant sense of adventure awaken.

"As you observe, and since we find ourselves in such a provocative and stimulating environment, it would seem a shame to sit passively at the Majestic waiting forlornly for what is certain to be more grim news from the Convent...Tell me what you have in mind, Juan Carlos."

"Well, on Friday I would like to take you to see the great pyramid at Chichen Itza. Along with la Virgen, it is among the most sacred sites in Latin America, and it would mean a great deal to me to share it with you, but since it will take a bit of time to make arrangements—a brief plane ride is involved—I suggest we first visit Casa Azul, the marvelous blue house of Frida

Kahlo here in the city. It is not an overstatement to say Kahlo, too, is a Mexican icon."

Lighting her second Deliciado, Frances inhaled and, refreshed, leaned back in the comfortable chair, "Of course, I wouldn't want to miss seeing Frida Kahlo's house, but tell me about this Chichen Itza. I regret to say I've never heard of it."

"Chichen Itza is an ancient Mayan complex in the jungle of the Yucatan with a monumental pyramid that rivals those of ancient Egypt," Juan Carlos informed his mentor.

"Once again taught by my students," Frances mused.

"Furthermore," he continued, "there are some very intriguing notions about the site that involve England and I think you may find surprising."

Now all ears, Frances leaned forward eagerly, "Please do go on...."

Juan Carlos proceded. "In the late nineteenth century, two pioneer British photographers and archeologists, Alice Dixon and her husband, Augustus Le Plongeon, explored the site, then still hidden in the jungle. As a result, they became proponents of so-called Mayanism. Among the first Europeans to photograph Mayan ruins, they promulgated the theory rather than Egypt, ancient Mexico was the cradle of civilization. According to the Le Plongeons, it was the Mayans who traveled from here to Egypt, thus explaining the remarkable cultural commonalities of the scale and design of the massive pyramids. Of course, at the time it was thought by some in ancient times the continents might have been closer."

"Extraordinary!" Frances exclaimed. "But why not? Unfortunately, I have never had the opportunity to visit Egypt and likely never will. Yet if somehow the ancient Mayans did make their way to the Middle East, that might mean the Hermetic tradition was transmitted first from Mexico to Egypt and from there made its way to Italy and via Bruno throughout Europe. What an astounding concept! And that interpretation also could account for Sor Juana's immersion in the Hermetic tradition. How incorrigibly Eurocentric I have been!"

Pleased he seemed to have snared Frances's interest, Juan Carlos added, "Recently the papers of Alice Dixon Le Plongeon have been uncovered at the Getty Institute in Los Angeles, and when she joins me, Petra and I intend to study and write about them. What's more, it seems there are several other early but largely unknown women explorers of Central America. We think one day it would be an interesting book."

Then unexpectedly, the handsome, young Mexican sat back in his chair, gazed at the tiled ceiling and began to lyrically recite:

"Beyond the blue, the purple seas,
Beyond the thin horizon's line,
Beyond Antilla, Hebrides,
Jamaica, Cuba, Caribbees,
There lies the land of Yucatan..."

Frances was enchanted. "How could I refuse such a marvelous invitation? And by the way are you the author of this intriguing poem?"

"No," Juan Carlos chuckled, "It is called 'The Hunter' by a British poet named Walter James Turner who was born in Australia of all places." Leaning forward eagerly, Juan Carlos inquired, "Then you are willing to undertake the somewhat arduous expedition, including a short trip in a small propeller airplane? It will take the entire day, although we should be back at the Majestic no later than seven."

"With the greatest interest and pleasure, my dear," affirmed Frances, who still relished the sensation of feeling her brain alight with new ideas and possibilities. "Yet we mustn't forget about events in the Convent. Hopefully by tonight or at least tomorrow evening there will be some new developments and insights. Certainly, today's unexpected display of raw emotion indicates the scenario is more complicated than first contemplated."

Chapter Thirty-Three

Later that day, along with Drummond and Elizabeth, who sat on either side, Guzman, at the head of the table, launched a series of interviews on more or less neutral ground. The refectory was several doors from the scene of the crime. Beginning with the Abadesa, each nun in turn was ushered into the room by one of Guzman's officers and invited to sit at the other end of the table. At Guzman's right hand the official translator took notes. In the meantime, Guzman had been informed by his assistants of a night watchman and handyman named José, who had been at the convent for years, along with his sister Maria who helped in the kitchen. Later in the day he intended to speak with them as well.

By the time she rejoined them, it was apparent the Abadesa had regained her equanimity. Taking her seat, she nodded and even managed to smile blandly while acknowledging her inquisitors who immediately had risen to their feet when she entered the room.

"Thank you for your cooperation, Abadesa," Guzman initiated the interview. "To begin, can you please tell us how and when you learned about the events in the library last evening? Then, perhaps, if you can, it would be helpful if you could provide a brief background of each of the *monjas* at San Jeronimo."

"Very well, I will do my best, Inspector," the Abadesa nodded. "Around ten last evening I was asleep in my chamber when someone knocked loudly at the door, which is very unusual. When I opened the door, I found Sor

Susana who was distraught. 'You must come quickly, Abadesa,' she sobbed, 'something terrible has happened in the library.'

"As soon as I found my robe, we ran to the library where immediately we saw Sor Angela on the floor. When I could find no pulse, we went to my office and called the police."

"What was Sor Susana doing in the library at that late hour, Abadesa? Is the library kept open at nighttime?"

"Although it is customary for the *monjas* to retire early, Inspector, in the spirit of Sor Juana, who often studied all night, the library is never locked. For that reason, after dark a small lamp on the desk is kept burning on the desk, Inspector. Since Sor Susana is somewhat of an insomniac, it was not unusual for her to be there looking for something to read."

"Can you tell us something more about her, Abadesa?"

"It is an interesting story, Inspector. Sor Susana's mother is an American nurse; her father, a Mexican, was a dentist here in Mexico City. Thus, Susana is bilingual. Before joining us, she studied library science at John Paul the Great Catholic University in San Diegò, so naturally, when she entered the Convent several years ago, I asked her to assist Sor Carmela in the library. It was she who encountered and brought the copy of the *Woman's Encyclopedia* back from California. The Convent is most fortunate to have her among us, as her professional training and language skills have proven invaluable to the organization and preservation of Sor Juana's collection. Visiting scholars especially are most appreciative of her knowledge and insights as well as cordiality. Indeed, given her devotion, poise, professional training, and language skills (she is fluent also in Latin and French), it is my hope when I am no longer able to carry out my duties Susana will succeed me as Abadesa."

"If I may, Inspector," Elizabeth interjected.

With a nod and an accommodating wave of his hand, Guzman indicated his permission for her to proceed.

"While it may not be relevant, Abadesa, do you happen to know why Sor Susana has difficulty sleeping?"

"In fact, Doctora, since we share the *problema*, Sor Susana and I often have discussed how best to deal with it. It seems when one's mind is overstimulated, it often is difficult to shut it down at night."

Elizabeth smiled, "I, too, am aware of the condition, Abadesa."

"For me," the cleric observed, "prayer, along with a cup of chamomile tea, is the best solution, but for Sor Susana it is books and more books—even if they frequently result in very late nights and very little sleep. The good news is Sor Susana keeps a diary of her reading and thoughts, which I hope she will one day leave to the collection, as Sor Juana did."

"What about the others, Abadesa?" Guzman returned pointedly to the focus of the investigation. Perhaps the librarian Carmela—was she in the library last evening?"

"To the best of my knowledge, she was not, Inspector," the Abadesa responded. "When Sor Susana and I discovered Sor Angela, no one else was in the library."

"Or at least you saw no one else, Abadesa," Drummond interjected. "A very good point, Inspector," Guzman confirmed. "Certainly, I suppose it is possible someone else could have been hiding in the stacks and left the library before my men arrived."

Here again—this time without asking permission—Elizabeth interjected, "Did Sor Carmela and Sor Susana work well together, Abadesa?"

"Another very good question, Doctora," Guzman affirmed, while Drummond smiled at her approvingly. "Well," the Abadesa hesitated, "the two are very different personalities, and while there is no overt competition between them, they are not what I would call close compatriots, Doctora."

"What can you tell us about Sor Carmela, Abadesa?" Guzman prodded.

"Sor Carmela has been at San Jeronimo almost as long as I have, Inspector. As it happens, our families are related, and we have known each other all of our lives. In fact, when we were still in our teens, our families arranged marriages to cousins, which we both found undesirable. So, following the example of Sor Juana herself and rather than openly defy our families, we decided to enter the Convent together. Since still today for traditional Mexican families a daughter or son who becomes a cleric is a badge of honor, convent life was an avenue of escape, and at the time each of us was attracted to the legend and—how do you say—*encanto* of Sor Juana."

Chapter Thirty-Four

Why over the years Carmela had become so hateful puzzled Teresa. Of course, she could understand her compatriot was disappointed not to be named Abadesa of the Convent, but her longstanding bitterness seemed to have become grafted to her soul.

Although their families were acquainted, they tended to travel in different social circles. Occasionally, Teresa had accompanied her mother when she called on Carmela's mother in their more or less humble home to discuss a matter having to do with the parent's association at St. Catarina's, the parochial school both girls attended. Although the visits had been cordial, Teresa's mother never failed to note how many religious icons adorned Carmela's home and how rigidly pious her stern mother appeared. Even a conversation over tea with cookies began with fervent prayer to the Holy Father.

"How on earth do children manage to breathe in that atmosphere?" she noted with disdain when they departed.

While the god of Carmela's mother, Juanita, seemed harsh somehow—despite the loss of a son to violence—Teresa's mother, Felicia, trusted a more compassionate and loving God. Whereas for her part, when her guests left, Juanita Hernandez complained about their perceived social superiority and self-righteousness.

"Who do they think they are, Carmela? Did you see how young Teresa copied her mother and patted her mouth with the napkin as if she was a great lady?"

Thereafter Carmela, who habitually licked her fingers while eating, never did so again and always used a napkin instead.

Ironically both young women entered the Convent of San Jeronimo in the same class. To her mother it wasn't a total surprise thoughtful, highly intelligent, and studious Teresa would choose to follow the example of illustrious Sor Juana rather than embark on university studies or a proper marriage to a carefully vetted, respectable suitor. As Teresa appeared to blossom and assume more responsibilities in the Convent, her mother was filled with admiration, pride, and even envy. A community administered by women appealed to her feminist sensibilities, and she was relieved—or so she imagined—Teresa would be spared the ravages of traditional Mexican patriarchy.

On the other hand, that repressed Carmela chose—or was urged—to forego worldly endeavors and passions and enter cloistered life was neither unexpected nor unwelcomed by her family. Yet her choice of the cosmopolitan Convent of San Jeronimo, rather than a more conservative order such as the Augustinian Sisters of the Recollect was puzzling.

What neither her preoccupied mother nor harried teachers recognized was, from her earliest years, young Carmela was riddled with insecurities. While competent, she never excelled academically and wasn't especially attractive like others of her more light-hearted classmates. What anchored Carmela was her mother's religious ferocity, which she absorbed like a veritable sponge, along with envy of Teresa Montoya, who seemingly excelled at everything and early on became a leader.

When it was announced Teresa had been accepted into the community of San Jeronimo and accolades rained down upon her, Carmela craved a taste of the same recognition. Although unfamiliar with the significance of Sor Juana's legend, why not follow Teresa's lead and apply for entrance into the Convent? Certainly that would be easier than striking out on her own somewhere else in the provinces. Furthermore, becoming a *monja* would please her mother and garner recognition for her family in the community. When Carmela proposed this idea to Sor Dorotea, who advised the young students regarding their future plans, she nodded with pleasure. Her less-than-outstanding academic record notwithstanding, the advisor assured Carmela she was certain, like most other convents in Mexico, San Jeronimo sought any and all applicants. Accordingly, she would urge her colleague and mentor Father Manuel Gonzales to meet later in the week with Carmela and write a recommendation for her.

Chapter Thirty-Five

When Teresa and Carmela began their novitiates, the Abadesa Concepción assigned Teresa to the library and her contemporary Carmela Fuera, who was less accomplished and personable, to a clerkship in her office. While Teresa immersed herself in the collection, studying all night and reading every volume, blossoming with knowledge, confidence, and poise, Carmela burrowed among papers and files. Developing a talent for numbers and strategy, she acquired an awareness of the workings of the Convent. Beavering away at her table in the corner of the office, she kept her head down while tuning into the Abadesa's meetings, thereby gaining insight into the organization and politics of the diocese.

Each week after his regular morning meeting with the Abadesa, the Cardinal's emissary Father Manuel Gonzales, who was a friend of her family and had sponsored Carmela's candidacy for San Jeronimo, invited her to join him and the Abadesa for coffee and a pastry in the refectory. Usually claiming she had much too much work to do (but really out of ennui with the tedious cleric's incessant nit-picking), the Abadesa declined Father Manuel's invitation but urged Carmela to accompany him. Over time, a sense of *comraderia* grew between the two *religiosos* into a kind of father-daughter relationship. Feeling significant for the first time in her life, Carmela trusted Father Manuel and willingly shared with him any information he requested regarding relationships and finances at the renowned convent, which, although declining in population, seemed to have reacquired prestige. Apparently, the notion of so-called women's liberation, anathema to the Vatican and especially the Mexican church's hierarchy, had garnered even more attention than ever to the audacious nun's story.

While several of the other *monjas* were older and had been in the Convent longer, a decade or so later when it came time for Abadesa Concepcion to retire, surprisingly, it was Teresa who with the approval of Rome was named by the Cardinal to succeed her. Since she had restored and reorganized the library and become a noted and knowledgeable guide to the collection for researchers from around the world, the president of the board of directors of the University, along with several prominent and significant donors to the diocese, recommended her to the Cardinal. When her appointment was announced, the Cardinal was flooded with letters of appreciation, which pleased the Vatican as well.

Although Carmela recognized she never was considered a candidate for the esteemed post of Abadesa, Teresa's triumph fueled her resentment and sense of inferiority. Over the years, the relationship of the two contemporaries had remained cordial but at times somewhat tense. Although in light of her longstanding service and diligence she was compensated with appointment as Teresa's replacement as head librarian, Carmela boiled with longstanding resentment. Continuing to meet each week with Father Manuel, unceasingly she criticized Teresa's management of the collection and reported for his consideration and review the addition of each and every volume to the collection. When the Spanish translation of *Giordano Bruno and the Hermetic Tradition* by Frances Yates arrived in the convent, Father Manuel was intrigued and borrowed the book to read and share with the Cardinal. A few weeks later, one volume in particular, donated by a university student who had recently returned from a semester studying in the States, shocked her, and knowing his likely reaction, she shared with Father Manuel a battered copy of *The Woman's Encyclopedia of Myths and Secrets* by American Barbara Walker. The illustrated and heavily annotated volume explored the origins of a matriarchal worldview, which the author claimed had been hijacked and suffocated by the patriarchal Judeo-Christian tradition. With competent English, Father Manuel quickly perceived the author's shocking premise, and as he leafed through the thick book, noting various pagan symbols, references to the Nag Hamadi manuscripts, and the long forgotten *Gospel of Mary*, a lengthy entry regarding Mary claiming her to be a personification of an ancient Great Mother, his face reddened, and his fingers began to tremble.

Boiling over, he raged, "This is blasphemy and has no place in the Convent!"

Snatching the book from satisfied Carmela's hands, he marched to the Abaseda's office to demand its immediate removal from the library. Accustomed to his outbursts, the Abadesa took the heavy volume from Father Manuel's trembling hands, and as he stormed off, calmly assured him she would deal with the problem. Later that evening in her chambers when Teresa began to examine the *Woman's Encyclopedia of Myths and Secrets*, she was never again the same.

Chapter Thirty-Six

"But somewhere along the way, for reasons I don't yet comprehend," the Abadesa continued, "Carmela seemed to turn away from Sor Juana's pursuit of the life of the mind and spirit and revert instead to more conventional and rigid patriarchal traditions. Perhaps it was Sor Juana's fervent feminism. In any event, I regret to say several years ago our views began to diverge and today are more estranged than ever. Indeed, on occasion she seems to have become critical of even our revered patron. Only a few weeks ago she went so far as to suggest if Juana had spent more time praying instead of reading, she certainly would have evaded the wrath of the Inquisition. As a result, she maintained, our order could have flourished, and today we would have more than a handful of *monjas*. Although in this modern day and age, when young women are worldlier, I think that is doubtful. *Por favor* among us, I believe Sor Carmela would prefer less notoriety for a martyred scholar and mystic and perhaps even another less tolerant and open-minded Abadesa."

"Perhaps someone like herself, Abadesa?" Elizabeth conjectured aloud, finding it impossible to restrain herself and not put into words what she thought the men at the table might be hesitant to say.

"Si, Doctora," the Abadesa nodded, "I regret to say that may be true, which makes me very *triste*—especially since our differences appear to have

121

adversely influenced the tranquility of the community. Frankly it has occurred to me at some point the Cardinal instructed Father Manuel to inform Sor Carmela if I were to retire or die she would be named Abadesa of San Jeronimo. Yet to my mind it would betray the spirit of Sor Juana if we were to succumb to the strict conservative and patriarchal views of the Roman Church. Therefore, rather than retire into seclusion and contemplation, which I long for, I have determined to remain Abadesa and maintain Sor Juana's legend as best and as long as I can—unless, of course, I am removed by the Cardinal."

"Sincerely I hope that does not happen anytime soon," Elizabeth stated directly to the Abadesa, who acknowledged the compliment with a slight smile while Inspector Guzman urged her to continue with her account of the other members of her community.

Chapter Thirty-Seven

"My assistant Sor Gertrudis has been at San Jeronimo for the past decade," the Abadesa continued her recitaton. "An unassuming young woman, she has found new life in the convent, and truly I'd be lost without her. A remarkably capable administrator and bookkeeper who is unfailingly calm and focused, she oversees the details of our day to day existence. Furthermore, over the years she also has found time to become a knowledgeable art historian, an *auto-didactica*, with a special interest in the work of Miguel Cabrera, who painted our renowned portraits of Sor Juana and *El Divino Esposo*. Lately, since we have begun to study the *Woman's Encyclopedia*, Sor Gertrudis has pursued other quite unorthodox avenues of thought regarding the paintings..."

"What about the painting, Abadesa?" Again, it was Elizabeth who pursued the Abadesa's line of thought.

Flushing slightly and somewhat reluctantly, the Abadesa began to explain, "Well, Doctora, the apparent androgynous qualities of Christ seemed to fascinate Sor Gertrudis, as they appear to conform to, shall we say, certain aspects of Ms. Walker's encyclopedia..."

"By any chance was Father Manuel aware of Sor Gerturdis's studies?" Elizabeth persisted.

Obviously becoming impatient with what he regarded as a distraction, if not trivia, Guzman once again redirected the interrogation while Drummond, too, became uncomfortable his wife seemed to be diverting the investigation toward irrelevant topics and indicated his concern with raised eyebrows.

"And young Sor Rosa—what can you tell us about her?" Guzman asked, ignoring Elizabeth's obvious vexation.

"Our youngest *religiosa*, Sor Rosa, an orphan, is just nineteen but has been with us for five years and adores everything regarding Sor Juana. Indeed, it sometimes occurs to me Rosa, who is a *prodigia*, envisions herself a reincarnation of Juana. In any event, she is steeped in her story, and because of her engaging personality and proficiency in English, I have assigned her the task of greeting visitors and conducting tours of the Convent."

"So she is familiar with the library and has contact with outsiders as well?" Guzman posited.

"Of course, Inspector, and Sor Juana's chambers as well."

"And what about the encyclopedia?" Guzman continued to probe.

"Sor Rosa has shown no special interest in the encyclopedia, Inspector. When not conducting tours, which are intermittent, she spends most of her time in solitude in her chamber, contemplating and reading her way through Sor Juana's entire library."

"Yet it is possible, isn't it," Guzman persisted, "Sor Rosa could maintain contact with a visitor to the Convent, Abadesa?"

"Theoretically, yes, but highly unlikely, Inspector," the Abadesa maintained.

All parties were taken off guard when—either intentionally or inadvertently—Guzman again abruptly changed course. Perhaps, Drummond observed, keeping subjects off-guard was Guzman's preferred method of interrogation, recognizing it could be an effective methodology.

"What can you tell us about Sor Angela, Abadesa? Why might she want to see the encyclopedia in the middle of the night, and, for that matter, was the book kept on the open shelves?"

"No, Inspector, to safeguard our only copy, I directed Sor Carmela to keep the *Woman's Encyclopedia* locked in the cabinet next to her desk in the library, along with several rare and fragile books that need to be protected and handled only with cotton gloves. As you witnessed this morning with Father Manuel's most regrettable outburst, the encyclopedia is quite controversial in the diocese, and I'd be dismayed if somehow it disappeared from the collection. Therefore, if a *monja* wants to examine it, she is asked to do so only in the library."

"Where is the key kept?" Guzman inquired.

"With others on a key rack hanging next to the door of the Chancery," the Abadesa replied.

"So it was readily accessible," Guzman pursued. "And was it there this morning?"

"Oh, dear," the Abadesa responded, raising her hand to her forehead, "in all the chaos I'm so sorry to say I've neglected to notice."

"Quite understandable and easy enough to confirm," Guzman assured the now somewhat frazzled administrator. "And is the door to the Chancery always locked?"

"Yes, Inspector, because my files contain highly personal information regarding our *monjas* as well as, shall we say, some controversial correspondence between the Cardinal and me. In the interest of history, I hope these records will be preserved, but in the meantime, I feel more comfortable locking the Chancery when I leave in the evening and take the key with me to my chamber."

"And do you think at some point Sor Angela might have taken the key to the desk in the library in order to look at the encyclopedia?"

"Not in my wildest dreams, Inspector!" the Abadesa exclaimed. "Sweet Angela was haunted by recurring nightmares of her dead child, killed in a terrible automobile accident that occurred while she was driving. Often she couldn't sleep and frequently went to the library to look for something to read to distract herself, enhance her prayers, and hopefully lull herself to sleep. If you were familiar with the provocative encyclopedia, I'm sure you would agree it's not the best book to promote spiritual tranquility."

"How horrible for her," Elizabeth murmured. As their eyes met, Elizabeth nodded sympathetically toward the Abadesa.

"Then how can we explain it was the encyclopedia and not any other book the deceased *monja* was clutching?" Guzman countered.

"I cannot, Inspector," the Abadesa replied forlornly, throwing up her hands and shaking her veiled head.

Turning toward his colleagues, Guzman conjectured, "If indeed that is the case, then it seems logical Sor Angelica is an unlikely thief, wouldn't you say?"

Since no one objected, he proceeded, "Therefore we must speak with the other *monjas* to ascertain their activities last evening. Furthermore, assuming it is missing, we must also determine the whereabouts of the key. With whom do you suggest we speak first, Abadesa?"

Before she could respond, this time it was observant Drummond who interjected, "If I may, Inspector. Abadesa, please tell us about your relationship with Father Manuel."

Obviously caught off guard and pausing to catch her breath, the Abadesa responded cautiously in measured words. "Father Manuel and I have worked together for many years on behalf of the Convent and diocese, Inspector, and at all times our relations have been, shall we say, sufficient."

"Then how do you explain his outburst regarding the encyclopedia?" Guzman took up the torch.

"Admittedly there are certain deviations from traditional doctrine Cardinal Mendoza and Father Manuel reject, but here in the Convent we are encouraged by Sor Juana's example of an insightful, inquisitive, and outspoken mentor to think for ourselves."

"Is this perhaps the *real* reason the encyclopedia was kept under lock and key, Abadesa?" Guzman countered.

"*Si*, Inspector," the Abadesa admitted. "Therefore, since it is our only copy, I thought it best to safeguard it in the cabinet and afford access to it only under supervision in the library."

"Then other than the two librarians, how would other *monjas* even know about the encyclopedia or its contents, Abadesa?" Guzman pursued astutely.

Quietly with a flushed face, the Abadesa responded, "On occasion, Inspector, the entire group meets to read aloud and discuss certain aspects of the encyclopedia."

Met with awkward silence of his colleagues, Guzman thanked the Abadesa and said, for today, he had no further questions for her.

"Very well, Inspector," but as she rose augustly from her chair, the Abadesa addressed him. "If I may, Inspector, I would like to make a request regarding Sores Maria and Lucia. If possible, I hope you might agree to speak with them at the same time."

As she explained, foundling identical twin sisters Maria and Lucia, who worked in the kitchen and garden and prepared meals for the community, were inseparable. Like medieval visionary Saint Hildegard of Bingen, they had been "gifted" by their state-appointed guardians to San Jeronimo nearly twenty years ago, soon after they had been discovered early one morning just outside the entry to the Convent. Bawling, entwined with one another, and wrapped in an indigenous blanket inside a wicker basket, the twins had known no other home. Unfortunately, she continued, neither girl showed the least sign of replicating either Hildegard's or Juana's brilliance.

"Truthfully, Inspector, I'm sorry to say both girls are limited intellectually and although they both can read, seldom, if ever, visit the library. Other than the kitchen or garden, they spend their time either praying in the chapel or the chamber they share. Since they are inseparable and emotionally dependent on one another, I feel it would be especially frightening for them if they were interrogated individually. Therefore, I wonder, if you must meet with them, I urge you to interview them together.

"Certainly, Abadesa, I will take your request under consideration," Guzman replied. "Still, in case they happened to have seen or heard something unusual last night that may be relevant to the incident, we must question them."

Chapter Thirty-Eight

After delivering Frances to the Majestic for siesta and ensuring she was safely settled in her room, Juan Carlos begged her to excuse him for the evening, as he was expected at a faculty meeting at the university. As he departed, he kissed her hand and informed her, after making arrangements for their trip on Friday to Chichen Itza, he would call for her at ten the next morning for their visit to Casa Azul. Although anxious for a debriefing by Drummond and Elizabeth, a few hours of solitude pleased Frances, who was terribly tired and needed time to process the distressing events in the Convent.

Understandably, the dinner convocation of the three traveling companions, who had determined to dine quietly, was a somber affair. Remarkably astute Jésus seemed immediately to perceive their subdued spirits.

"May I bring some *jerez, mis amigos?*"

"Yes, please, Jésus, along with some guacamole, and then, if possible, we'd like some time before ordering our dinner," Drummond assumed command.

"*Claro, señor.*"

Jésus quickly returned with four, small crystal glasses of sweet, amber sherry and a warm bowl of creamy, green guacamole with multi-colored tortilla chips, which immediately helped boost their spirits. Absurdly, she realized, in light of the grim events of the past twenty-four hours, Frances was reminded of communion wafers and the similar effect they frequently had on her.

Like a priest, Drummond raised his glass and acknowledged, "Certainly none of this expected this sordid turn of events on our holiday, but it has

129

been my experience the passions that give rise to them are universal and thus can be encountered anywhere and at any time."

"Still another example, Stuart, of the universality of human emotions," Elizabeth suggested.

"Indeed, my friends, yet in a convent and especially the sacred refuge of Sor Juana de la Cruz they seem especially tragic," Frances lamented, as she sipped some sherry and dipped deeply into the irresistible guacamole.

"For that matter, Dame Frances, think what happened last year at our beloved Warburg," Elizabeth reminded them. "Perhaps as we did then, here in Mexico, working together we again can put the pieces together to solve the puzzle. What are your observations so far, Stuart?"

"I think, my dear, once again your legal mind has focused our attention where it belongs, which is on solving this case as quickly and efficiently as possible," Drummond responded. "Initially in this instance, since we are dealing with a cloister and much smaller cast of characters, it appears there are fewer suspects than there were last year at the Warburg."

Retrieving a notebook from her purse, Elizabeth proceeded, "Let's list them as best we can recall. For starters shall we consider the Abadesa herself?"

"Of course, she too." Drummond asserted without hesitation.

"And Father Manuel?"

"Yes," he stated curtly.

"And what about the nuns?" Elizabeth persisted. "Although we met some of them today and you met with them yesterday, Dame Frances, I wonder if you have any insights regarding their character or possible motives."

"While to say the least it was challenging to be in the company of a cadre of women all dressed alike, in fact, I couldn't help but form a few initial impressions," Frances revealed.

"Please share them with us, Dame Frances," Drummond urged.

Sipping a few more drops of sherry, she leaned back and opined, "Well, to begin and in no special order, it is apparent the Abadesa and Sor Carmela are two strong personalities who, one can surmise, may not always agree with one another."

"If ever," Elizabeth, per usual, interjected.

"Secondly, poor deceased Angelica seemed to me just that, angelic, as she softly strummed her guitar while we sang hymns together. Truly I was moved to tears. That she may have been apprehended stealing any book from the library seems improbable to me, as does the possible culpability of the two young twins. As you have reported, it is acknowledged they are simple girls who never step foot in the library and care little for anything other than their kitchen and garden. Which leaves the two assistants, bilingual librarian Susana and the Abadesa's assistant Gertrudis...."

"But why would any of them be in the library at night?" Elizabeth persisted.

"Indeed," Drummond agreed. "According to the Abbess, after dinner a Great Silence ["*Magnum Silentium*," Frances amended] is customary in the Convent. At that time, the nuns return to their cells for prayer and contemplation. Yet two added facts are relevant: The women are not mandated to remain in their cells *and* the library is kept open at all hours."

"What's more, Stuart," Elizabeth noted, "poor Sor Angelica, who suffered from insomnia, was known to frequent the library at all hours."

"Since there appears to have been a struggle," Frances resumed, "it seems obvious someone else was in the library at the time, but for what purpose? Isn't that the real mystery we're facing?" she queried.

"Indeed, Dame Frances," Drummond confirmed. "Heightened by the revelation, as Elizabeth noted and we learned today, apparently all is not harmony and devotion at the convent. In fact, the tension between the Abadesa and the librarian Sor Carmela is palpable."

"Remarkable!" exclaimed Frances, recalling poor, dead librarian Pratt at the Warburg, "Another disgruntled librarian here in Mexico...Really and with no intention to diminish the tragedy, I'm beginning to think librarians are another endangered species," prompting ironic smiles from her colleagues.

"By the way, and perhaps of added relevance, having spent several hours with them yesterday, I'm now fairly certain it was Sor Carmela who was missing from the Abadesa's Eucharist. Do you think this might be interpreted as an indication she neither approved nor wished to participate in the unorthodox ritual?"

"Very interesting indeed," Drummond noted. "I'll be sure to inform Inspector Guzman about this in the morning."

"But come to think of it, Stuart, did anyone today even mention the feminist ritual Dame Frances witnessed? And in light of the focus on the encyclopedia, don't you think that's peculiar?"

"Not really," Drummond conjectured. "Even assuming the Abadesa were trying to keep the ritual secret from the Cardinal, it may not be relevant to Sor Angela's demise."

"In any event," Frances, who had been cogitating the scenario while continually munching chips, resumed, "Don't we also have to consider what the thief planned to do with the encyclopedia?"

"What are you suggesting, Dame Frances?" Drummond leaned forward.

"Well, assuming the culprit was one of the *religiosas*, what was she planning to do with the encyclopedia once she took it? Destroy or hide it in the Convent? And if so, how and where would she do that? After all, it is a sizeable volume...."

"Or perhaps," Elizabeth quickly pursued Frances's line of thought, "do something else with it...."

"Such as?" Drummond queried, looking from one to the other and marveling at the ingenuity of his two astute female colleagues who seemed to be channeling one another's observations.

"Precisely," Frances nodded. "Assuming it *was* one of the nuns, wouldn't it be more likely she was planning to deliver the book to someone outside the Convent for its disposal?"

Whereupon immediately Frances and Elizabeth locked eyes and simultaneously exclaimed, "Father Manuel!"

"If you will excuse me, ladies, I must make a phone call," Drummond announced as he rose abruptly from his chair and left the table.

Chapter Thirty-Nine

At 9:00 A.M. on Friday, a stern, if not ferocious, Father Manuel arrived at the Convent and entered the refectory. Sixtyish and stocky with short-cropped salt-and-pepper gray hair, he was attired in a traditional black suit with *rabat* and white clerical collar. As he entered the room, acknowledging his station, Guzman, Drummond, and Elizabeth rose from their seats, although no handshakes were proffered. Indicating the empty seat at the end of the table and for the official record Inspector Guzman presented his colleagues along with the translator and stenographer of the proceedings.

"Because of his experience with Scotland Yard, I have asked Inspector Drummond, who is visiting Mexico, to assist with the investigation," Guzman explained, "and since his wife, Doctora Wolcott, is an attorney, I feel it is appropriate to ask her to attend our interrogation of the *religiosas*."

The priest harrumphed.

Guzman continued, "As you know, Father Manuel, we are here to investigate the unfortunate death in the library Wednesday evening of Sor Angela. Regrettably it appears her death may have involved foul play."

"Certainly, Inspector, both the Cardinal and I are deeply distressed about this incident, which reflects ill on both the Convent and the diocese. While it further concerns us that visitors, no less foreigners, are privy to the unfortunate events, as well as the investigation," the priest nodded toward Drummond and Elizabeth, "the Cardinal has instructed me to assure you we will do all we can to cooperate and resolve the unfortunate affair."

"Very commendable, Monsignor," Guzman replied. Then adopting a tone that struck all parties as quite aggressive, he abruptly launched the interrogation with a startling questioning. "Can you tell us, Father, why the sight of the book Sor Angela was holding made you so angry when you saw it?"

Drummond recognized the ploy. *Catch them off guard*, he noted with admiration.

Flaring immediately, Father Manuel reddened and slammed the table with his right hand. "That filthy book has been banned by the Cardinal and therefore has no place in this or any other house of worship in Mexico! What on earth does it have to do with your investigation, and why are you asking about it here and now?"

Coolly Guzman persisted, as with raised eyebrows Drummond and Elizabeth exchanged glances. Seasoned investigator Drummond noted the Mexican's *froideur* and persistence.

"Why do you find this book—indeed, any book in the Convent library—such a threat, Father?"

Now barely able to contain himself, Father Manuel virtually shouted, "Because it is blasphemy! Questioning the origins of the Bible and the story of Christianity itself by suggesting instead absurd notions of matriarchy is outrageous! Furthermore, I have been informed the outlawed Women's Ordination Conference has infiltrated the convent, and rituals are conducted here according to its tenets—by women no less! *Any* ritual that deviates from tradition will *not* be tolerated in Mexico!"

"The Inquisition lives in modern-day Mexico," Elizabeth muttered and shook her head while making a note to share details of the interview with Frances.

Aware he had touched a nerve and perhaps even a motive, Guzman prodded and pursued his prey, "The Women's Ordination Conference, Father? I'm not familiar with that organization. Can you tell us about it?"

"It is a group of Catholic women here in Mexico, Europe, and America who argue women should be Catholic priests, which of course violates all Church teachings. Truly it is preposterous, as well as unacceptable!"

"How do you know the conference is active here in the Convent, and if indeed that is the case, how did you learn about it?"

Suddenly Father Manuel seemed to regain a degree of self-control and awareness of the implications of Guzman's questioning. "There can be no secrets in the Convent, Inspector."

"Then it was the Abeseda who informed you?"

"I will not disclose my sources to anyone but the Cardinal, Inspector."

"Even if a question of murder may be at issue, Father? To the best of my knowledge, even the Church is not above the law in Mexico."

The priest flushed, stared ahead, and said nothing.

Since Frances had recounted in habitual detail the riveting story of her experience in the Convent, Elizabeth and Drummond knew it could not have been the Abesada who disclosed the existence of WOC at San Jeronimo.

Elizabeth mulled to herself, "Ah, the plot thickens...later we must be sure to share this twist with Dame Frances for her further consideration."

Guzman persisted, "Doesn't it seem to you more than mere happenstance the victim was clutching the controversial volume regarding feminist theology?"

"I have no further thoughts along these lines to share with you, Inspector," Father Manuel asserted.

"Then let us try to focus on the circumstances of the death of Sor Angela. When did you last visit the Convent, Father?"

Still obviously uneasy, Father Manuel responded, "Usually I visit the Convent Monday afternoons to meet with Abadesa Teresa."

"And do you visit the library to meet with Sor Carmela as well?"

"Yes, Inspector, the integrity of Sor Juana's collection is vital to the reputation of the Convent."

"And at any time did either librarian Sor Carmela or Sor Susana inform you the library had obtained a copy of the *Woman's Encyclopedia of Myths and Secrets* and the Abadesa ordered it kept locked in the library desk?"

"They did not," Manuel asserted, although Elizabeth was certain she saw him squirm in his chair, and with a raised eyebrow indicated as much to Drummond.

"Which I suppose would explain your anger and surprise when Dame Frances uncovered the book in Sor Angela's arms." Guzman seemed to throwing Father Manuel a lifeline of sorts to which he appeared to clutch eagerly.

"Precisely, Inspector."

"Thank you, Father. That will be all for today," surprising all parties, Guzman terminated the interview. Later his tactics would become more apparent...

Chapter Forty

As the library was closed during the investigation and the questioning continued in the refectory, Sores Gertrudis and Susana met in the garden to have a heart-to-heart talk and compare notes regarding their interviews. Over the past decade the two *monjas*, who shared similar upbringings and suffered setbacks that led each to convent life, had bonded and become confidants. The focus of their reading and studies complemented one another and stimulated both. Susana was an ardent feminist who advocated for women priests while Gertrudis was immersed in a quest to decipher the underlying meaning of Cabrera's provocative art, as exemplified by his two stunning paintings in the Convent. Certainly, in *El Divino Esposo* the artist was expressing notions of ambiguous sexuality, which intrigued Gertrudis and, if she allowed herself to pursue the thought, appealed to her senses as well.

Both in their forties with good heads on their strong shoulders, their positions as administrative assistants to the Abadesa and convent librarian, also had afforded them significant insights into the dynamics of the convent. Mutual concern for the welfare of the sanctuary and its inhabitants, along with perpetuation of the legacy of Sor Juana, motivated both *religiosas* and inspired their studies and prayers.

With an American mother and Mexican father, Sor Susana Martinez grew up in two worlds—really three if her Jewish heritage were taken into account. During the Holocaust, her father's parents, along with a number of their congregation in Budapest, had immigrated to Mexico. At the time, as illustrated by the devastating experience of Jewish passengers on the *St. Louis*, the ship was turned away from the coast of Florida. Ironically, archly Catholic Mexico seemed a more welcoming destination. Furthermore, it was easily accessible to the United States via California, and the weather was more agreeable than that of Canada, where many other Jewish exiles found refuge. Upon arrival Susana's grandparents changed their surname from Lowenthal to Martinez.

Totally bilingual in English and Spanish, yet not entirely comfortable in either milieu, that Susana would become a member of the community at San Jeronimo astonished her family and friends and sometimes even herself. Her mother, a nurse, and her father, a dentist, trained and met at the Great Catholic University of San Diego, where two decades later their daughter studied library science. Although each the first of their families to attend university, neither parent urged their daughter to follow their trades. Pointedly her father, an ardent auto-didact of history and literature, discouraged it. A talented amateur actress, her mother would rather have been on the stage than tending patients.

Though nominally Catholic, Elena and Enrico Martinez disregarded church doctrine, autocratic priests, and notions of pervasive sinfulness. Instead, religious holidays were devoted to lavish meals with pitchers of sangria rather than remorse and piety. Generally, they ate their way through concurrent Jewish and Christian holy days, savoring matzo ball soup with jamón at a festive Easter/Passover dinner, accompanied by *panes dulces* and pitchers of sweet sangria.

To ease their children's way, Elena and Enrico Martinez determined the British American School afforded them both quality education and exposure to multi-layered facets of Mexican society. Once when she complained to her mother about the complexities of her heritage, Elena proffered two pieces of advice Susana never forgot: "First, stop whining, and two, turn it around: You can go anywhere!"

Although their son became a medical doctor, from her earliest days it was apparent precocious Susana was a budding scholar. Whenever she visited her beloved grandmother's library in Rancho Santa Fe in California, she gobbled up children's books she found on the shelves. Few little Mexican girls read the enchanting tales of Pollyanna and Heidi. Since both parents were voracious readers, Susana also had access to books in both languages at home and was invited to read any that appealed to her. Shakespeare's plays were a family favorite and often read aloud on Sunday afternoons.

Yet her fiercely feminist mother insisted Susana have a career. Even if she were to marry and have a family, every woman should be able to be independent and care for herself. Library science seemed a natural fit.

Thus, it came as a surprise to both parents when teenage Susana began to attend weekly Mass. Although slim and conventionally pretty, unlike her classmates at the British American School in Mexico City, Susana disdained slumber parties, movies, and rowdy boys. Even a thoughtful and mannerly young male classmate, who occasionally called on her and brought fragrant bouquets of lavender and daisies, bored her to distraction. Her brother's young children interrupted and annoyed Tia Susana.

Instead, she preferred to read in her bed under a handwoven Mexican blanket, as she often did late into the night. On a school trip to el Convento San Jeronimo, she was enthralled by the library of Sor Juana de la Cruz. Thereafter she began to imagine a life of solitude, removed from cares of daily tedium, surrounded by stacks of books rather than pots and pans, diapers, and laundry.

Chapter Forty-One

At the university library in California, one volume especially transformed Susana's worldview. *The Woman's Encyclopedia of Myths and Secrets* by American scholar Barbara Walker revealed a heretofore unknown world of feminist spirituality and matriarchal traditions. Searching for what she did not know when she attended Mass, that she might combine her studies with spirituality inspired by a Great Mother enveloped Susana with a sense of serenity, purpose, and destiny. When she shared the volume with her mother and talked of her reverence for Sor Juana, Elena, too, understood, affirmed, and even envied her daughter's decision and determination to lead a life of the mind and spirit, providing, of course, first she obtained her degree in library science.

Thus, when she completed her studies in library science graduating at the top of her class, Susana applied for admission to the Convento San Jeronimo. Upon acceptance by the community and immediately assigned to assist in the sacred library, novitiate Sor Susana felt she had found her calling and never once looked back.

When she wasn't praying, studying Scripture, or trying to sleep, which she considered a waste of time, beginning with Sor Juana's writings and poetry, Susana determined to read her way through the renowned Convent's reassembled collection of several thousand volumes. As if led personally by the mystical scholar and *monja*, she soared from theology to philosophy and history and stories of earlier religiosas, such as Teresa of Avila and Ursuline

Marie Madeleine Hachard of Louisiana. Retracing Juana's intellectual journey, Susana learned about Greek goddesses Ceres, Hecate, and Proserpina, and among others, studied the writings of German Jesuit Athanasius Kircher and Mexican polymath Siguenza y Gongora. Remarkably Kircher propounded the theory Ancient Egypt was the font of Indian, Chinese, and Mexican civilizations.

Always Susana cross-referenced her readings with entries in the *Woman's Encyclopedia,* which she had brought with her to the Convent.

As she reread and absorbed them over the years, the nearly one thousand lines of Sor Juana's celebrated poem "Primero Sueno" had become another bible of sorts for Susana. Composed more than three centuries earlier, the writings of the enlightened *religiosa,* heralded by some observers as the first feminist of the New World, enabled Susana to process her own complicated heritage. Somehow Juana's illegitimacy enabled her to embrace her mixed heritage and deepened her appreciation of her Mexican milieu. Sometimes, like Juana, Susana wondered in which world she belonged. Above all, Juana's struggle with gender issues—especially regarding the Church—seemed as complicated and relevant in the closing years of the twentieth century as they were in the 1600s. *Entre mas cambian las cosas, mas siguen igual,* she frequently mused.

Chapter Forty-Two

To mark her forty-seventh birthday, Susana asked the Abadesa if she might be excused from her duties in the library for the day. At the same age—after her books had been taken away—Sor Juana succumbed to the plague while comforting and caring for other *religiosas* as they too died. Her request, granted at once by empathetic Teresa, was motivated by a strong urge to retreat to Sor Juana's chambers to contemplate and pray.

At six the morning of her birthday, Susana woke refreshed from a few hours of unusually sound sleep. She wrote, as Juana had done each day, a few lines in the journal she kept by her bed to record her dreams (She had dreamed of two young girls running through a field of wildflowers: Were they she and Juana?), washed her hands and face, and wearing a simple, white cotton gown, a short, white veil over her head, and soft, felt slippers, climbed the stairs to Juana's chambers. There on the wooden altar before Cabrera's illuminating portrait of the brilliant mystic, Susana found a silver goblet of sweet wine and a plate of communion wafers the Abadesa had placed there for her the night before. With gratitude and tears in her eyes, Susana ingested the Eucharist and sat on the bench facing the portrait and, gazing into the eyes of her mentor, began to contemplate and pray.

With her she had carried a worn paperback copy of the Penguin edition of Sor Juana's poems and letters with facing pages of Spanish and English translations. Always it was interesting to discern how the words spoke differently to her in each language. In all likelihood, her exposure to student activists in California rendered Juana's feminist assertions better suited to English, yet in either version the nun's bold questions in *A Spiritual Self-Defense* fired Susana's own resistance. *Three hundred years later!* she marveled.

Like men, do women not have a rational soul? Why then shall they not enjoy the privilege of the enlightenment of letters? Is a woman's soul not as receptive to God's grace and glory as a man's?

On the other hand, *El Primero Sueno* regarding Juana's spiritual journey had to be absorbed in the original tongue. Enhancing the delight of the soaring verse were the goddesses Juana employed to personify the flight of the Soul, and for Susana, Thetis, Venue, Persephone, and Proserpina became cherished companions. For Juana the Night was feminine, and as she retreated with the colorful dawn, like Juana, centuries later Susana's "external senses were reactivated with an affirmation that left the World Illuminated, and awake."

At the same time, Juana brilliantly articulated the life of the mind and the flight of the spirit. Since neither depended on the teachings of the Church, it was no wonder the Inquisition raged at the outspoken scholar. At two in the afternoon after hours of contemplation, when she felt calm and satiated, Susana left the cloister and placed a small bouquet of wildflowers on the grave of her heroine, who was buried in the courtyard.

There she pondered further, "Since it appears I will be given more years than Sor Juana, I wonder, dear Mentor, what my mission entails...."

Chapter Forty-Three

Over the decades, each book led to the next, and as she progressed into the eighteenth and nineteenth centuries, Susana also became intrigued with the struggle for independence throughout Latin America. Along with the terrible upheaval of the Mexican Revolution in the first decade of the twentieth century, the conflict between church and state permeated the violent history. As a result, and based on the recommendations of visiting scholars, volumes along these lines were added to the library's collection.

When it was published, Octavio Paz's stunning biography *Sor Juana, or The Traps of Faith* electrified Susana. Over and over again she poured through the pages until they were worn and smudged, which was how Sor Susana, and in turn the Abadesa, encountered Frances Yates.

Among other revelations, Nobel Laureate Paz extolled the British scholar's renowned study of martyred Catholic priest Giordano Bruno and what Yates identified as the Hermetic tradition. That a century before Sor Juana an Italian priest proselytized spiritual notions remarkably similar stunned Susana and at once she acquired a copy of *Giordano Bruno and the Hermetic Tradition* for the library.

Thus it was in the Convent where promising young scholar Juan Carlos Ortiz, too, was introduced to Bruno and Frances Yates and, thanks to a fellowship from his university, made his way to the Warburg Institute in London. While Juan Carlos was in London, Susana, who was eager to share Yates's insights with the Abadesa, began to translate *Giordano Bruno and the Hermetic*

Tradition into Spanish. Although the Abadesa's English was competent, Susana thought the nuances of Frances's elegant writing would be difficult for her to appreciate. Over the next year, chapter by chapter, she shared the translation with the Abadesa, who was equally enthralled and enlightened.

Before the project was completed, the Abadesa declared, "We must invite Dama Francesca Yates to visit us in the Convent—if that is, she would agree and is able to travel halfway round the world to Mexico."

Chapter Forty-Four

Quiet, orderly, cloistered life surrounded by books suited Susana perfectly. Assigned to assist Sor Carmela in the library, she approached her position with diligence and enthusiasm. Anxious to apply the skills she had learned in her library courses, she quickly determined the card catalog must be revised. To her astonishment she discovered any book title beginning with "The" was shelved under "T," which meant *The Last Days of Tenochtitlan* and *The Life of Saint Teresa of Avila* were found next to one another.

"Incredible!" Susana exclaimed when she realized the blunder and reported it to Sor Carmela, who mumbled a lame excuse.

Unfortunately, the crusty supervisor who had reigned over the library for nearly two decades neither comprehended the issue nor—even if and when she eventually did—had any intention of revising longstanding arrangements with which she was completely comfortable. She knew just where to find each and every volume. Unfortunately, any request from a visiting scholar to study a specific title at a nearby table tended to annoy her—to say nothing of a young upstart who talked of introducing modern methods to reorganize and track the rich collection!

Perceiving the problem and in order not to vex Carmela or jeopardize her time in the library, Susana, while familiarizing herself with the collection, determined to keep her head down and focus instead on assisting scholars with their research. Diligently, she retrieved requested volumes and replaced them on the shelves at the end of the day, while on a manual typewriter she re-constructed the catalog and re-organized the library into appropriate topics so one day another librarian (hopefully named Susana) could more easily enhance its relevance and value.

Each week when the Cardinal's lieutenant, Father Manuel, visited the library to chat with Sor Carmela, Susana greeted him dutifully and then found an excuse to disappear into the stacks so the two longtime cohorts could confer regarding news in the Convent.

But the day the Abadesa instructed Sor Carmela to add the *Woman's Encyclopedia of Myths and Secrets* to the collection, as Susana's mother would say, "All Hell broke loose!"

After leafing through just a few pages, Carmela turned bright red and demanded of the Abadesa, "Where did this heresy come from, Teresa? Do you really intend to add it to the sacred library? If so, you have gone too far!"

"Indeed, Carmela, I have studied the volume carefully. Since it is both scholarly and insightful, I am convinced Sor Juana herself would approve, but for safekeeping please keep it locked in the desk drawer and allow only readers I approve to examine it. As you know, the key is kept on the wall in my office," she added as, winking discreetly at Susana, she swept from the library.

Witnessing the contretemps from the table where she was sorting through notes and papers for the archives, Susana kept her head down and prayed to the Great Mother she hadn't jeopardized her cherished position in the library or—Heaven forbid—even in the Convent! What was she thinking when she presented the book to the Abadesa? Although the Abadesa received the book graciously and with great interest, how could Susana have been so naïve as to think it wouldn't offend traditional Catholics? What if Sor Carmela shared it with her confidant, Father Manuel?

Chapter Forty-Five

The art of Miguel Cabrera saved Sor Gertrudis Jimenez from a life of quiet despair. The nearly forgotten next to last of an undisciplined pack of seven children born within a decade, at an early age Gertrudis retreated into silence. Led by a bullying older brother, the cacophony at the evening dinner table in central Guadalajara was overwhelming. Her harried mother struggled to feed and maintain some sense of order over her chaotic household while her grim, accountant father presided over the table in stony silence. After helping with the pile of dishes, Gertrudis quickly retreated with a book to the top of the bunk bed in the small, cluttered bedroom she shared with her older sister Alicia.

Neither especially pretty nor especially plain, Gertrudis found her parochial school, where she earned adequate grades, more or less satisfactory. At least it was orderly and calm. Fortunately, one class taught by Sor Lucretia, a young nun from the Sisters of Mercy in Mexico City, was revelatory. Following a field trip to view the stunning murals by Jose Clemente Orozco at the Palacio de Gobierno, Gertrudis was enthralled. Like those of Orozco's contemporary Diego Rivera, the vibrant murals depicted chapters of Mexico's violent history. The tour guide boasted their scale rivaled those by Michelangelo in the Sistine Chapel!

Awash with color, passion, and fury, the murals both entranced and unsettled young Gertrudis, new sensations she had never before experienced. Thereafter, after school, whenever she wasn't expected at home for endless mundane chores, she found her way to the chapel, only a few blocks from school. Among the tourists she would lay back on a stone bench gazing at the magical vaulted ceiling, yet still something was missing. It wasn't until a subsequent search among the art books in the school library she discovered her passion: *El Divino Esposo* by Miguel Cabrera. Who was this alluring Christ, and what mysteries did he conjure? A mesmerizing spiritual yearning was awakened in young Gertrudis. Yearning to be enfolded in his arms among the fragrant blossoms, for the first time in her young life Gertrudis experienced passion.

Then when she turned a page and encountered Cabrera's portrait of Sor Juana de la Cruz, Gertrudis recognized a heroine whose story, when she learned it, afforded a new world and possibilities. Upon learning both paintings were housed in the Convent of San Jeronimo in Mexico City and recognizing such an adventure was beyond the comprehension of her beleaguered parents, Gertrudis dared to turn to the only person who might appreciate her excitement. Would Sor Lucretia be able to suggest some way she might travel to Mexico City to see the paintings in person?

Recognizing and identifying with the young girl's ardor, a rarity among her mostly indifferent students, Sor Lucretia stated, "Of course, Gertrudis, I will take you there myself."

With her parents' permission and gratitude for the opportunity, Gertrudis spent her first weekend ever away from home and traveled by bus with Sor Lucretia to Mexico City. At the invitation of Abadesa Teresa, they spent two days and nights in the Convent participating in the daily rituals, awash in the spirit of Sor Juana and the art of Miguel Cabrera. Upon returning to Guadalajara, Gertrudis announced to her parents next year, when she received her high school diploma, she would enter the Hieronymite Order of Sor Juana de la Cruz in Mexico City.

Chapter Forty-Six

During one of her sleepless nightly forays in the library, it was Susana who had discovered Angela's lifeless body, and visions of the scene continued to surge through her head, exacerbating her insomnia. At first, she had assumed it was an accident—that Angela had tripped and fallen or perhaps had a seizure of some kind. When it was revealed Susana was clutching the sequestered *Woman's Encyclopedia of Myths and Secrets*, more macabre thoughts aroused suspicions, which she shared in the garden with Gertrudis.

"What if it weren't an accident, Gertrudis? What if someone wanted to harm sweet Angela? And if it *is* foul play, who in the Convent could be involved?" she pondered. "Certainly neither Maria nor Lucia is a likely suspect, and now that I think about it—between us, please— we mustn't consider the Abadesa either...or should we?"

"Carmela," Gertrudis stated matter-of-factly.

Stunned, Susana responded, "But why? Although her anti-feminism is blatant and her lack of graciousness glaring, beyond refusing to attend the Abadesa's Eucharist, why would she need to go to the trouble of removing the encyclopedia from the library?"

The two nuns continued their stroll among the bed of pink dahlias, yellow marigolds, and lush, dark green hostas.

When they reached the herb garden, Gertrudis said matter-of-factly, "Politics."

"Meaning what, Gertrudis?"

"At some point soon, Susana, the Abadesa, who is not getting any younger, will retire—unless, Goddess forbid, she becomes ill. Then, if the diocese determines the convent is to remain open, someone is going to have to take her place. Personally, I hope and pray it is you, Susana, but there is no doubt in my mind Carmela covets the position. Therefore, it occurs to me she and Father Manuel, and through him the Cardinal, could have some kind of agreement along these lines. Perhaps removal of the encyclopedia is part of a plot to undermine the Abadesa, or if it could be used as evidence of disobedience, even the future of the Convent as well."

"Great Mother, I hope and pray you are wrong, Gertrudis! Do you think we should share these thoughts with Inspector Guzman?"

Chapter Forty-Seven

The convent was the only home Sores Maria and Lucia had ever known. Since they never knew their young mother, who deposited the twin infants at the door of the convent one dark night twenty years ago, the twins were raised and coddled by a cadre of loving nuns. From their earliest awareness, they had been sheltered in the kitchen, which became their haven, while the Convent garden was their playground. Of course, the Abadesa insisted the girls be taught to read and write, but along with their tutors, she recognized neither was inclined to follow the illustrious path of Sor Juana; yet as soon as they were handed large mixing spoons and bowls instead of toys and dolls, they were delighted with pastry dough and never seemed to tire of other kitchen chores, picking vegetables, and arranging fruit plates. The kitchen was spotless—even washing dishes seemed to give the twins pleasure—and something fragrant and enticing was always stewing on the ancient wood stove.

As they matured and were permitted to handle knives and cut vegetables, it quickly became apparent to Sor Catalina, who oversaw the kitchen, the twins were gifted in another way, destined to become accomplished, creative chefs. As Catalina aged and was no longer able to manage the kitchen, quite confidently the twins assumed responsibility to feed the *monjas* three times a day, year in and year out. With herbs, fruits, and vegetables from the garden drying on hooks on the walls, another creation rising in the oven or a tempting *cazuela* bubbling on the ancient stove, the *cocina* became a kind of chapel. Frequently the *monjas* and other guests stopped by to commune with its identical twin priestesses, who never failed to share samples of their artistry, as if their samples were communion wafers.

Soon after he began his weekly visits to the Convent, Father Manuel discovered the wonders of San Jeronimo's vegetarian kitchen and thereafter conveniently scheduled his visits to coincide with the midday mealtime. Although habitually he consumed meats with gusto, the twins enticed him with various delicacies. Seemingly simple dishes, such as chunks of melon with fresh mint, hard-boiled eggs in aspic, and *arroz con queso*, were mouth-watering. Fresh *naranjada* pressed from the fruit of two orange trees in the garden was virtual ambrosia, but above all, their desserts and pastries were divine!

Just the thought of their *tres leches* cake, *pan dulce, conchas de colores*, or *flan chocolate* made the priest's mouth water. Since Monday was Father Manuel's usual day in the Convent, the menu that day always included one of his favorite desserts. After his weekly meal in the refectory, when he stopped by the kitchen to compliment them, the twins basked in the glow of his effusive praise. Yet it was the Abadesa's compliments after the luncheon for the old English woman that gave them even more pleasure.

"*Muchas gracias, mis queridas*, today you have outdone yourselves. Now please join us for the Eucharist; the dishes can wait for a while."

Having been raised among a cadre of caring women, it never occurred to either twin there was anything unusual about the feminist ritual.

Later that evening as they washed the dishes and made preparations for breakfast next morning, it was unsettling, even frightening, to think they heard heavy footsteps on the back stairway outside the kitchen. At any time, the presence of a male in the convent was unusual. As she held her finger to her lips, Lucia peered through the crack in the kitchen door and saw a male figure in dark jacket and trousers climbing the stairs to the library. Could it be Father Manuel? Although she wasn't sure, Lucia closed the kitchen door, and clutching hands, the sisters huddled together behind the butcher-block table in the center of the room.

"What shall we do?" Maria whispered.

"Nothing that I can think of right now," Lucia cautioned, "other than get to our room as quickly and quietly as possible and then first thing in the morning report the event to the Abadesa."

Chapter Forty-Eight

While Drummond, Elizabeth, and Guzman interviewed suspects in the Convent, Juan Carlos and Frances arrived via taxi at Coyoacan, one of oldest districts in Mexico City, where Frida Kahlo's colorful blue home was a principal attraction. As they drove through the charming bohemian neighborhood, Juan Carlos related the extraordinary story of the assassination in 1940 of Leon Trotsky, who was seeking asylum from Stalin in Mexico City.

"Remarkable!" Frances declared, "It is terribly embarrassing how little I know about history!"

Her former student laughed out loud. Frances wasn't sure what to expect and was chagrined further to admit she wasn't familiar with Kahlo's story, although Elizabeth raved about her art. Today anything that diverted Frances's thoughts from the tragedy in the Convent was worthwhile, and since Juan Carlos was proving an exemplary, informed guide, she was eager for adventure.

The modest, square adobe house on the corner, where Kahlo was born, lived with her husband, Diego Rivera, and died, wasn't merely blue; it was a startling cobalt blue. Immediately Frances was intrigued, but when she entered the courtyard garden, overflowing with ferns and giant pots of vibrant, colorful flowers, she was enchanted. When they entered the simple kitchen and began to view the collection of Kahlo's unique and challenging art, Frances was enthralled.

Even more remarkably, one self-portrait in particular, hanging on the wall of the living room instantly reminded Frances of Tarot! Certainly, *Las Dos Fridas*, which portrayed different aspects of the artist's personality, thus, like the cards, providing insights into her worldview.

The Two Fridas by Frida Kahlo

"Always," Juan Carlos explained, "Frida portrayed herself in colorful *china poblana* style that honored indigenous women. Conveniently it also provided *camuflaje* for Frida's crippled leg, injured in a terrible accident when she was a young girl."

In Frida's bedroom, the underside of the canopy over the bed, covered with a handwoven blanket, was decorated with more painted images intended to enhance the artist's dreams.

"How charming and very Tarot!" Frances exclaimed. "Perhaps I'll try that in my bedroom at Claygate."

As distracted as she was by Kahlo's exotic art, at the same time Frances realized she couldn't stop thinking of events in the Convent. As the self-portraits conveyed different aspects of Frida's politics and complicated personality, couldn't they, like the Tarot, also afford insights into the personalities of the nuns at the Convent? If so, perhaps this approach could help solve the mystery of Sor Angela's death, as they had at the Warburg last year.

In another remarkable self-portrait created in 1937, Frida, again wearing *china poblana*, portrayed herself holding a handwritten love note to Trotsky. Before his assassination in their kitchen, the infamous communist lived in exile with Kahlo and Rivera.

"Once again the intersection of art and politics," Frances observed as she gazed in wonder at the riveting painting. "As with Renaissance art and the Tarot, the history of Mexico, which I am determined to explore, is told by its artists, and in this case, as with Sonfinisba Anguissola and Lavinia Fontana, another remarkable woman experienced it firsthand."

At the crammed gift shop, along with a tea towel depicting the luscious ripe watermelons of Frida's *Viva la Vida* for Ruby, Frances was in the process of purchasing a catalog of Frida's art for the Warburg when she spotted a deck of Tarot cards illustrated with Frida's art.

"Eureka!" she exclaimed as she added the cards to her printed shopping bag. Perhaps, she conjectured, this evening at the hotel, as they had done last year in London, she, Drummond, and Elizabeth could examine the cards for possible clues regarding the cast of characters in the Convent.

Perceptively gauging priorities, Juan Carlos suggested a special spot for their lunch.

"Marvelous!" Frances exclaimed as they entered rustic Cantina la Guadalupana, an unimposing adobe red brick building on a narrow cobblestone street a few blocks from Casa Azul. Surveying the vibrant scene enhanced by servers dressed like Frida in *china poblama* and several waiters in sombreros, Frances sensed immediately, "It exudes history!"

As Juan Carlos informed her, the cantina was founded in 1932, and soon became the favored meeting place of Frida Kahlo, Diego Rivera, and their circle of artists and agitators, who dined there frequently.

When they were seated side by side at a narrow table along the dark wood wall, which was cluttered with paintings and local mementoes, a handsome server in a red matador's jacket arrived to take their orders.

"May I suggest a mojito, Dama Francesca? Made with lime juice, soda, and fresh mint, it is remarkably refreshing. Usually it is served with rum, but without liquor it is still a most refreshing drink."

When their drinks arrived they were accompanied by a platter of *botanas* ("appetizers" Juan Carlos noted). This time with no dire after-effects, another sweet, fruity potion delighted Frances. Although she gleefully eyed a bowl of fresh, bright green guacamole, she was encouraged by her host to sample other mouth-watering local delicacies, such as *jicama*, a fried sweet potato served with slices of lime.

"Delicious—another perfect choice!" Frances grinned, as the sweet potion slid over her dry tongue and parched throat.

"I am so pleased," her young host responded, as he sipped a cold cervesa. "But tell me, please, what did you think of Frida's art?"

Staring into space and reflecting for a moment, Frances responded thoughtfully, "Steeped, as I have been all my life in art of the European Renaissance, Frida Kahlo's art is a revelation to me. So much so that it will take further study and time to process its impact. Yet, as with the Tarot, I am struck with the universality of her images and symbols and the fact that art can speak directly to each of us regardless of our origins. Clearly she was a genius."

"*Claro*, I couldn't agree more!" Juan Carlos confirmed. "Although my own studies also focus on earlier times, the early years of the twentieth century in which Kahlo and Rivera flourished are among the most vibrant in Mexican history."

"Of course, the premise of Aby Warburg's library was the relationship of art and history and the spiritual insights art can provide," Frances added. "Tell me, Juan Carlos, do you think, like Tarot, Frida's art can tell us anything about events in the Convent?"

"What an intriguing idea!" Juan Carlos reflected. "I must admit I'd like to know what is happening and how our colleagues are managing the crisis."

"As would I, my friend," Frances nodded solemnly, as she sipped her soothing mojito.

Chapter Forty-Nine

Meanwhile in the Convent, growing increasingly provocative, the interrogations continued. With an obvious and proverbial chip on her shoulder, testy Carmela virtually marched into the refectory and other than a glare offered no response to Inspector Guzman's greeting, "Thank you for joining us, Sor Carmela."

Recalling the Abadesa's account, Elizabeth couldn't imagine being expected out of any sense of tradition or family obligation to marry someone she didn't love. *What does this say about Mexico?* she pondered, as gratefully she gazed across the table at her handsome new husband, focused intently on the proceedings.

The renowned convent had offered a respectable avenue of escape from sexual slavery and domestic tedium, and early on Carmela, who was bright and ambitious, had determined to make the best of her stark but sheltered circumstances. Unlike her contemporary, Teresa Montoya, she hadn't entered San Jeronimo out of any yearning for spiritual enrichment or haven or even admiration for sainted Sor Juana.

Begrudgingly, she had to admit over the years more perceptive and self-righteous Teresa had outsmarted and outmaneuvered her by skillfully and always graciously navigating church politics. Above all, she championed Sor Juana de la Cruz, who—after publication of the Paz biography and the stunning Mexican documentary *I, the Worst of All*—had become a modern feminist icon.

For these reasons Cardinal Mendoza's predecessor had named Teresa Abesada of San Jeronimo.

Aware she was far from scholarly, when it was offered as a form of compensation, Carmela calculated if she couldn't be *abadesa*, the position of librarian of the convent would afford a measure of prestige. More significantly, overseeing the priceless collection was the next most prestigious position in the Convent. Furthermore it afforded Carmela contact with church hierarchy, visiting influential scholars and inquiring tourists. All the while professionally educated Sor Susana ran day-to-day administration of the library.

Yet that her contemporary Teresa managed to outmaneuver her by becoming *abadesa* was an unending source of irritation for Carmela. Everyone who met her seemed to succumb to Teresa's poise, intellect, and attractive appearance, all of which admittedly she lacked. For as long as Carmela could remember she had engaged in a losing battle with a hot temper, reflected in her pursed lips, clenched jaw, narrow eyes, and general dour demeanor. Since she first became a novitiate, this trait was noted on each and every one of her yearly evaluations filed with the diocese.

Carmela's interview with Guzman, Drummond and Elizabeth fulfilled all of these stereotypes.

"Thank you for meeting with us, Sor Carmela," once again Guzman opened the session.

There was no response.

Edgy, Elizabeth immediately concluded. "Were you in the library Wednesday evening?"

With no eye contact, Carmela stared ahead and responded icily, "I was not."

"Are you familiar with the *Woman's Encyclopedia of Myths and Secrets*?"

"I am."

"When did you last see the book?"

"When Sor Susana took it to the Abadesa's meeting with Profesora Yates Wednesday afternoon."

"Where is it kept in the library?"

"As the Abadesa ordered, the encyclopedia is kept in a locked drawer at the desk in the library."

"Do you have a key to the desk?"

"I do not; it is kept in the Abadesa's office."

"So when someone wants access to the book, they first must stop at the Abadesa's office."

"That is correct."

"When did you leave the library on Wednesday?"

"After the meeting with Profesora Yates, I tidied the space and returned to my chamber."

"Did you join the others for supper in the refectory?"

"Yes."

"And then?"

"I returned to my chamber for the evening."

"What do you think of the *Woman's Encyclopedia*, Sor Carmela?"

At last a reaction! Flaring, Carmela virtually hissed, "It is heresy and has no place in this library!"

"Did you ever share your feelings about the book with the Abadesa?"

"Many times, Inspector."

"And she disagreed?"

"The book is still here, Inspector."

"How do you explain the fact Sor Angela was clutching the book?"

"I cannot," she glared into space.

"When was the encyclopedia added to the collection?" Elizabeth, increasingly impatient with the huffy nun, couldn't sit still any longer.

Turning toward her, Carmela responded, "When Sor Susana entered the convent with her own collection of books. I believe she brought the book from the United States."

Determining to maintain the pressure, Drummond followed suit. "How often does Father Manuel visit the library, Sor Carmela?"

All three parties watched with surprise as the librarian's face turned bright red.

Aha, a nerve—good for Stuart! Elizabeth nodded approvingly toward her perceptive husband.

Quickly recovering, Carmela responded calmly, "On Sundays, when he conducts the Mass for us, and then usually once during the week to meet with the Abadesa regarding Convent affairs."

"Does he visit the library as well?" Guzman followed Drummond's lead.

"Usually, yes."

"Why?"

"Well, I suppose to survey the state of the collection."

"Does Father Manuel know about the encyclopedia, Sor Carmela?"

For the first time the seemingly self-assured nun hesitated and looking down, murmured, "I don't know...."

Chapter Fifty

After a brief but delicious lunch of warm tacos stuffed with beans, avocado, and shredded cabbage, cold glasses of freshly squeezed lemonade and paper-thin almond cookies, prepared and served at the table by Sisters Maria and Teresa, the afternoon interviews were a welcome change of tone.

With a high forehead and wide, dark brown eyes, soft-spoken and poised, Sor Susana, more handsome than pretty, appeared to be somewhere in her forties. Perhaps a legacy of her American mother, her complexion was paler than those of her colleagues. Combined with traces of indigenous heritage, the effect was intriguing. As she entered the refectory, Elizabeth liked her immediately.

Taking the place indicated by Inspector Guzman, Sor Susana placed her hands left atop right on the table and, never moving them, in a firm, well-modulated voice calmly and confidently responded to Guzman's questions.

"Sor Susana," he began, "Please recount the circumstances of your presence in the library last evening. Why were you there, and about what time did you discover the body of Sor Angela?"

"Certainly, Inspector," Susana soberly began her recitation. "Frequently in the evening I visit the library. As you may know by now, the library is never closed or locked. Since I often have difficulty sleeping, I have found quiet and browsing through the collection for another book to read helps ease the path to slumber, but last evening when I entered the library—about nine, I believe—I noticed right away something was amiss."

"What was that, Sor?" Guzman urged.

"Usually a lamp is kept lit on the desk, but last night the room was totally dark. At first I assumed a bulb had burned out and started to walk to the closet behind the desk where the bulbs are kept. That's when I stumbled and fell over dear Angela's body. Of course, at first I didn't realize what it was or that it was she...it was ghastly." Susanna's voice cracked and momentarily she lowered her head.

Reminded of Dame Frances's similar encounter last year at the Warburg with the lifeless body of the dead librarian, Elizabeth shook her head, *Really such incidents shouldn't happen to sheltered, scholarly, and religious women and especially not in hallowed libraries!* she silently grieved. *This seems to be a pattern on both sides of the Atlantic.*

"Quite understandable, Sor," Guzman consoled the disturbed nun, "Please take your time."

"Thank you, Inspector, I am recovered." Susana quickly reassured the audience.

"And what did you do then?"

"When I stood, I went to the light switch by the door. When I turned it on and saw Angela on the floor, I thought she might have fainted and tried to awaken her. When I could not and thought she might be dead, I ran out of the library to the Abadesa's chamber. She was sleeping but quickly dressed and together we returned to the library. When we determined Angela indeed was dead, we went immediately to the Abadesa's office and called the police."

"Did you see or hear anything or anyone else in the library?"

"No one, Inspector."

"And did you then wait for the police in the Abadesa's office or did you return to the library?"

"We thought it best to wait in the office, Inspector."

"Then theoretically, Sor Susana, someone else could have been in the library and waited for you to leave before exiting?" Drummond interjected.

"Very good point, Inspector," Guzman acknowledged. "And did you happen to notice Sor Angela was clutching a book?" Guzman resumed the lead. "I did not, although now I recall her arms did appear to be entangled in her habit," Susana responded.

"Is there any reason you can suggest why the book she was found to be holding was the *Woman's Encyclopedia of Myths and Secrets*? Are you familiar with the volume?"

"Of course, Inspector, it is I who presented it to the library. Furthermore, I am pleased to report it has become the primary reference source for our knowledge of the Great Mother."

"Did Sor Angela share those sentiments?"

"Si, Inspector, in the Convent we regularly acknowledge our reverence for Her."

"In spite of traditional Catholic teaching, you too are comfortable with that concept—the worship of a female deity?"

"Completely, Inspector, such worship doesn't preclude the notion of God the Father as well. Frankly I don't understand what my, or for that matter, what Angela's theology has to do with her death," Susana challenged Guzman, turning the table of the interview. Amused, Elizabeth acknowledged and smiled at the clever nun, who obviously was growing impatient with the ennui of the interrogation.

Good for her! Elizabeth cheered to herself. *Although I'm frequently accused of seeing it everywhere, do I perceive a hint of sexism in the Convent? If not, why is this line of questioning relevant?*

Apparently realizing he had veered off course and been checked, Guzman retreated. "I understand it was you who introduced the encyclopedia to the Convent...."

In a reference lost on her audience, Susana acknowledged, "*Si*, Inspector, as Sor Juana said about herself, it was 'I, the Worst of All,' who purchased the book in California and brought it with me to the Convent. In the spirit of Sor Juana, I determined the encyclopedia should become a part of her collection and—of course with the approval of the Abadesa—be made available to the members of the community. At the risk of, as we say, *enganos de grandioso* it even occurred to me Sor Juana herself would have appreciated the volume!"

"Can you tell me something about the encyclopedia and why you think it would displease the Cardinal?"

"Because in sum, Inspector, it is an overtly feminist book that espouses a matriarchal rather than patriarchal worldview. Therefore, it contradicts everything the hierarchal Church in Mexico, which is very, very conservative, stands for. The thought of any significant role for women in the Church is anathema to Cardinal Mendoza and Father Manuel, who obediently and unfailingly follows his orders.

Chapter Fifty-One

Compared to the initial interviews, fortuitously the meeting with Sor Gertrudis was relatively brief and cordial. Quickly it was determined Gertrudis, who served as administrative assistant to the Abadesa, spent her spare time studying the two remarkable Cabrera paintings in the library and Sor Juana's quarters. With a soft voice, a more or less plain face, and gentle demeanor, Gertrudis responded readily to all questions. No, she was not in the library Wednesday evening. After the meeting with Frances, she, too, had dined with the other *monjas* and returned to her chamber for the evening. Yes, she was familiar with the encyclopedia and participated in the feminist ritual led by the Abadesa. Of course she was a feminist, she asserted as if surprised anyone would bother to ask! But her real passion was the art of Cabrera. Although she found the encyclopedia worthwhile, her studies pursued another avenue.

With the exception of a pimply, gawky neighbor with bad breath, Gertrudis had neither serious suitors nor an interest in acquiring any. When she first learned about Sor Juana de la Cruz at the convent school she attended in Guadalajara, Gertrudis aspired to join the community at San Jeronimo and learn as much as she could about the woman who chose the life of the mind and spirit over an arranged marriage. The solace of convent life suited her perfectly.

With no illusions she ever could equal her heroine's intellectual accomplishments, Gertrudis spent hours studying the Cabrera portrait in Juana's chambers and believed through Cabrera's art she had acquired insight into her heroine's worldview.

What interested Gertrudis especially was the time-honored myth nuns were the brides of Christ. To Gertrudis, who rejected the concept intellectually, it seemed improbable intrepid Sor Juana embraced the notion. Accordingly, Gertrudis's studies led her beyond the *Woman's Encyclopedia* to works such as *Brides of Christ* by Asuncion Lavrin, another book she valued highly. Had the tradition evolved, she wondered, to teach young girls to be submissive or to assuage them for bypassing marriage and children? Did the young brides experience sexual ecstasy, as *El Divino Esposo* implied? After years of study, Gertrudis had to admit the image of a sensual, inviting Jesus caused her heart to skip a beat and made her blush. Occasionally she even imagined herself in the arms of the exotic young Savior. What had she missed?

Chapter Fifty-Two

Holding hands and wide-eyed, the identical twin nuns entered the room and immediately Elizabeth's heart ached for them. In their habits it was impossible to tell them apart. Obviously terrified, they sat side by side, clutched one another's hands, and looked down at their laps.

Poor darlings, they look like two identical dolls, Elizabeth sympathized as Guzman gently began his questioning in Spanish.

"Thank you for meeting with us, Sor Maria, Sor Lucia, these are my colleagues, Doctora Elizabeta Walcott and Inspector Drummond, and we would like to ask you a few questions about events in the Convent Wednesday evening."

Neither nun reacted in any way or showed the least change in facial expression as Guzman proceeded.

"Please tell us about your activities in the Convent Wednesday evening."

After a few seconds Sor Maria looked up quizzically and quietly responded, "In the kitchen, Inspector?"

Guzman nodded "*Si.*"

In a barely audible whisper, Maria began, and the translator relayed to Elizabeth and Drummond, "As we do each evening, we prepared and served dinner to the Abadesa and other *monjas* here in the refectory."

"Were all of the *monjas* present at dinner?"

"*Si*, Inspector."

"And after dinner—what did you and Sor Lucia do?"

"We washed the dishes and made preparations for breakfast and set the table as we do each night."

"And at what time did you conclude your duties?"

"Usually we are finished by eight, Inspector, and then return to our chamber."

Although fairly certain of their response, Guzman nevertheless felt constrained to ask, "Do you ever stop by the library after dinner?"

Both nuns blushed, lowered their eyes and shook their heads, "We do not read many books, Inspector," Lucia volunteered.

Nevertheless Guzman continued his inquiry. "On the way to your chamber, do you walk in the hallway alongside the stairway to the library?"

Both nuns nodded.

"And on Wednesday evening, by any chance did you see anyone on the stairs?"

Looking at one another out of the corner of their eyes, while reaching under the table to clasp hands even more tightly, both nuns uttered a silent "*Si.*"

Instantly straightening in his chair and peering over his glasses at the two *monjas*, Guzman continued, "Can you provide any description at all?"

Shaking her head, Maria still in a whisper responded, "In the evening it is very dark in the hallway, Inspector. The figure was near the top of the stairs when we saw it, so we are not sure who it was...."

"Although we couldn't see his face," Lucia added, "it appeared to be a man wearing trousers."

"Trousers or overalls?" now hot on the trail, Guzman leaned forward and pursued. Aware a significant development in the investigation could be unfolding, Drummond and Elizabeth sat straighter on the edges of their hard, wooden chairs and awaited a translation.

"Dark trousers, Inspector," Lucia commented softly. "Workmen are never allowed to enter the Convent in the evening."

"Then do you have any idea who the visitor could be, Sisters? Who has access to the convent in the evening?"

"Of course, who can visit is determined by the Abadesa, Inspector, but there are seldom any visitors in the evening. Occasionally Father Manuel joins us for dinner, and last week," she said, nodding toward them, "Señor Cruz dined with the Abadesa in the refectory to discuss preparations for the visit of the visitors from Inglaterra."

At the mention of Juan Carlos's name, alarm bells clamored in the heads of each of the three inquisitors.

Not dear Juan Carlos! Elizabeth prayed. *What would he be doing in the Convent in the middle of the night?*

Simultaneously both seasoned professional detectives pondered, *Although unlikely, you never know...and for that matter, where* was *Juan Carlos last evening? Why hadn't he joined them for dinner?*

"What did you do then, Sores?" Guzman continued. "Did you report the visitor to the Abadesa the next morning?"

"No, Inspector," they responded, shaking their lowered heads. "We returned to our chamber, said our prayers, and since we didn't understand it, decided it best to keep the matter to ourselves."

"Thank you, Sor Maria, Sor Lucia," Guzman closed the interview. "You have been very helpful."

Still holding hands, the twins scurried from the refectory, while Guzman wondered aloud to Drummond and Elizabeth whether it had occurred to either twin a notice to the Abadesa might have prevented a death in the Convent. Yet even now, in light of their obvious naiveté and innocence, he doubted whether the threat of possible danger occurred to either *monja* or troubled them in the slightest.

Chapter Fifty-Three

The day's interrogations completed, the two detectives and one attorney sat back and assessed the situation. Only with considerable self-restraint did Elizabeth refrain from uttering one of her favorite lines from the Coen brothers' riotous film *Burn After Reading.*

"So what do we have here?"_

"Obviously, the dynamics in the Convent are more complicated than one would expect in a cloistered religious community of women," Guzman observed.

Considering the circumstances and although she felt herself bristle, Elizabeth managed to hold her tongue and not say what she was thinking, *Just among women? Of course, nothing like this could ever happen among monks in a monastery!*

Reading her thoughts and appreciating her discretion and self-control, Drummond came to the rescue. "As in any case, wouldn't you say, Inspector? It seems the death—or, let's be candid, likely murder—could involve powerful political interests beyond the Convent."

"Indeed, Inspector," Guzman concurred, "The current ecclesiastical regime appears to be engaged in a campaign to restore a conservative worldview here in cosmopolitan Mexico City."

"Especially when it comes to women," Elizabeth, who no longer could restrain herself, was compelled to add.

"Unfortunately that, too, seems to be the case, Doctora," Guzman acknowledged. "Do you agree, however, while we have a great deal to sort out here, the twin *monjas* seem not to be involved directly in the death of Sor Angela?"

"Other than their negligence, Inspector," Elizabeth noted somberly.

Nodding to Elizabeth, Guzman abruptly changed the subject and inquired of Drummond, "At risk of appearing frivolous, *mis amigos*, I wonder if it would be inappropriate to suggest a diversion this evening."

"What is that, Inspector?" both advisors inquired.

"As it happens, and while admittedly it is short notice, which I regret, tonight is the monthly meeting of the Lautero Lodge here in Mexico City. It occurs to me—if, that is, you have no other plans and the Doctora and Dama Francesca would excuse us—you might care to join me, Inspector. It would be an honor to introduce you to my compatriots while further discussing today's developments in light of your important call last evening. Lautero is the oldest Lodge in the country, and several illustrious Mexicans have been members."

Seeing Drummond's eyes light up, Elizabeth immediately consented. "Please, gentlemen," she urged, "feel free to enjoy your meeting. It would be a unique experience for my husband, and gladly I will spend—in fact relish—a quiet evening at the Majestic with Dame Frances. In light of today's meetings, there is a great deal to discuss with her."

"*Gracias y muy geneoso, Doctora.* Then perhaps, Inspector, if he has no other plans, you can invite Juan Carlos Ortiz to join us as well. He seems to be a fine young gentleman, and the Lodge is always looking for new members."

Chapter Fifty-Four

Seated companionably side by side at a table against the wall and—except for solicitous Jésus—without male company, Elizabeth and Frances dined indoors at the wood-beamed Majestic dining room. Once again, sensing their somber mood and without being asked, perceptive Jésus brought two delicate crystal goblets of amber, sweet sherry and made recommendations for their dinner: a warm chicken casserole with *macaronnes* and mild *queso* for Frances and baked tilapia with a fig sauce for Elizabeth.

"*Gracias,* Jésus," Elizabeth acknowledged as Frances leaned back against the banquette, sipped some of the sweet sherry, licked her lips, and sighed.

"The dire circumstances notwithstanding, I must confess, Elizabeth, it is a pleasure to have you all to myself this evening. Admittedly it has occurred to me this week has been far from the usual carefree honeymoon!"

With an ironic smile Elizabeth nodded, "As always, the pleasure as well as privilege are mine, Dame Frances, but, yes, to say the least it has a unique, sobering, although quite provocative honeymoon."

Somewhat assuaged and brimming with curiosity, Frances inquired, "If you can, please tell me what you learned today at your meetings in the Convent."

"Well, to begin, Dame Frances, and beyond issues raised by the presence of the encyclopedia, it seems the dynamics in the Convent are quite complicated. To put it mildly, all of the Sisters do not love one another or live in peace and harmony."

"Unfortunately, I am not surprised. On Thursday morning one could sense the tension—especially between Sor Carmela and the Abadesa. By the way, I have replayed the scene in my mind and believe it was Carmela who was absent from the Eucharist service Wednesday morning.

"Yet I must say, quite adamantly and convincingly, Carmela insisted she was not in the library Wednesday evening when poor Angela was murdered. Actually, that makes sense to me," Frances noted, as she aggressively dipped a blue corn chip into the large bowl of guacamole Jesus had placed on the table between them—with a side dish of fiery red salsa for Elizabeth.

"Why is that, Dame Frances?"

"Well, originally," Frances opined, "if the goal was to remove the encyclopedia from the library, I thought someone—shall we say Sor Carmela—had simply to hand the encyclopedia to Father Manuel, but upon reflection, there seems a more convenient and logical solution: What if the desk had been unlocked earlier, so all Father Manuel (or someone else) would have to do was open the unlocked desk and remove the book whenever he or she arrived in the library? If that were the case, no one would have to be in there to meet and hand over the book."

"Brilliant per usual, Dame Frances!" Elizabeth exclaimed. "The minute he returns from the Lodge, I must tell Stuart. Of course, if that is the case, it wouldn't relieve the person who opened the desk of culpability."

"*Claro*," Frances nodded, snaring another of the fast-dwindling supply of chips.

Chapter Fifty-Five

As their fragrant, hot dinners arrived along with two glasses of La Tente rosé and a pitcher of sparkling water enhanced with slices of lime, the intriguing dialog continued.

"But what about the presence of the Women's Ordination Conference here in Mexico? Do you think the death in the convent is related to its practice there? And if you don't mind my asking, Dame Frances, how do you feel about the issue?"

"As you are aware, I am certain, Elizabeth, I am a relative latecomer to feminist theology and historiography, yet thanks to Director Hilb, who discovered the *Woman's Encyclopedia* and introduced me to a group of dissident feminist Catholics in London—to say nothing of visions of an androgynous Christ in Tarot, my sense of a patriarchal worldview has been expanded."

"Speaking of Cabrera's *Divine Spouse*!" Elizabeth noted.

"Touché!" Frances laughed with relief. "On this lighter note," she suggested, "despite dour events in the convent, do you think it would be terribly inappropriate if we endeavored to discuss the arts as well this evening? Truly I was overwhelmed by the sights I saw today at the Casa Azul."

"Yes, please, let's change the subject," Elizabeth readily agreed, as she sampled the divine, perfectly cooked fish. "Although I've visited the house on an earlier trip, I so hope I'll have a chance to share it with Stuart before we leave for home."

"Lovely." Frances leaned back against the banquette and breathed a sigh of relief. "If we could, I also would like to hear your views on Sor Juana and the impact of the Cult of the Virgin on Mexican culture and their relationship, if any, to the unique art of Frida Kahlo as well."

"What a difficult assignment, Dame Frances!" Elizabeth laughed. "But, yes," she continued, "I have been thinking along those same lines and hope to pursue the topic further when we return to the Warburg, but, first, if I may, I have a question for you: Are you surprised by the apparent influence of the Hermetic tradition here in Mexico?"

Without hesitation, Frances responded, "Quite honestly, Elizabeth, I am overwhelmed by it! To encounter the spirit of Bruno and the universal church across a vast ocean and continent is a stunning revelation that reaffirms my devotion to Bruno's message. Furthermore, as illustrated by the omnipresence of the Virgen of Guadalupe, the notion of a female deity is deeply ingrained into Mexican culture. As Elizabeth the Virgin Queen appreciated her lasting hold over her followers and made brilliant use of the Virgin Mary's mystique and iconography, both icons stand in stark contrast to centuries of pervasive and rigid European patriarchy. Even more provocatively, today's visit to the Casa Azul enhanced my impressions...."

Digging into her sack, Frances retrieved the catalog she had purchased at Coyoacan and showed it to Elizabeth. Opening to the page she had marked with a postcard, she displayed Frida's extraordinary *The Two Fridas*. Although the faces were identical, one Frida was portrayed in *china poblana* and the other in European dress. Holding hands with their hearts connected by a common red blood vessel, the painting afforded insights into the various facets of Frida's complex personality.

"As a result, it occurs to me even supposedly tranquil, cloistered nuns, whose individuality supposedly has been erased by veils and long dark robes, have complicated personalities."

"There is no doubt in my mind, Dame Frances, while varying circumstances led each of them to convent life, the nuns share the same weaknesses and passions we all do. While far from typical, surely there can be no better example than the Cabrera's *Divine Spouse*!"

"Touché, my dear!" Frances laughed, then continued, "As we toured the extraordinary house filled with Frida's revelatory art, it also recalled complex Tarot images and occurred to me we might garner insights regarding the suspects in the Convent from the images of the self-portraits. As we did last year with the Tarot, Frida's portraits can be read and interpreted. What's more, Frida's identity with indigenous culture illustrates the overt syncretism that is so apparent and striking in Mexico. Our most informative guide explained Frida dressed in local costume as a sign of solidarity with women of a region called 'Teuantepec,' which is reputed to have been a matriarchal society."

Leafing through the catalog, Elizabeth stopped at the striking self-portrait of Frida with a small portrait of Diego Rivera implanted at the center of her forehead. Somehow the image disturbed her. Why wasn't her husband's portrait over the artist's heart? Then she saw the caption noting the painting was created during the couple's divorce proceedings.

"How sad," she reflected, "but how interesting, Dame Frances. It says here both Frida and Diego Rivera had a Jewish parent, who immigrated to Mexico in the early twentieth century. Surely this influenced their art and worldview while introducing still another facet to the syncretic complexities of Mexican culture."

"I couldn't agree more," Frances affirmed. "The painting calls for further study when we return to the Warburg. In fact, I have been thinking perhaps it calls for another seminar."

"Oh, I hope so! It's a wonderful idea," Elizabeth urged.

Frances's seminar regarding Tarot was a highlight of Elizabeth's studies at the Warburg.

"Somehow Stuart and I *must* find time to visit Casa Azul before we leave. Really, along with tragic events in the Convent, there's too much to do in Mexico! Which reminds me, I know you must be tired, but if you're willing and able to wait a bit longer to get to your room...."

Frances nodded, "Of course, my dear, I confess I am grateful to have you all to myself this evening."

"Thank you, I too cherish our time together," Elizabeth teared as she clasped Frances's hand. Then reaching into her own sack bag, she withdrew two worn books. "Yesterday instead of siesta Stuart and I decided to do some exploring and discovered divine Under the Volcano bookstore on Calle Celaya not far from the Zócalo. Although I loathed the movie with Albert Finney, the shop, named for Malcolm Lowry's novel, specializes in English translations. Apparently, there is a market here for Anglophone literature, which is still another intriguing aspect of the city. In any event, I found another book, a novel regarding Mexico by a Scottish woman, and I would like you to have it. It is a story about the Emperor Maximillian and the Empress Carlota. How I wish I had the opportunity to read it before visiting Chapultepec!"

"Still another!" Frances exclaimed, as she leafed through the pages of a worn copy of *The Cactus and the Crown* (1962) by Catherine Gavin. "What a lovely souvenir and gift! I will begin reading it tonight."

Then Elizabeth opened a volume of Sor Juana's poems translated into English, which she informed Frances she intended to donate to the Warburg collection, and as the two colleagues sat quietly side by side, began to read softly a poem titled "You Foolish Men."

You foolish men who lay the guilt on women,
Not seeing you're the cause of the very thing you blame;
If you invite their disdain with measureless desire
Why wish they will behave If you incite to ill.

Chapter Fifty-Six

Wrapped in his traditional apron and with a ritual handshake, Hermano Pedro Guzman greeted Drummond and Juan Carlos at the door of the elegant Lautaro Lodge.

As he handed him a guest Masonic apron, Guzman drew Drummond close and whispered, "The matter you called about last evening has been addressed, Inspector. Please be certain to thank Dama Francesca for her insights and assistance."

Drummond nodded grimly. Then Guzman welcomed Juan Carlos, and as they approached the darkened, richly wood-paneled ritual chamber, pointed out the portrait of Mexican revolutionary, Catholic priest, and Freemason Miguel Hidalgo, who led his followers under the banner of Our Lady of Guadalupe. Although Drummond had heard of Hidalgo, he hadn't realized he also was a priest. When Guzman shared details of his execution in 1811, at once Drummond thought of Giordano Bruno. *Like Bruno, another martyred priest—how can their messages be so threatening to the powers that be?*

Portraits of other renowned Latino Freemasons lined the walls: Bolivar, San Martin, O'Higgins, etc.

Surprised to see a portrait of the Italian patriot Garibaldi, Drummond asked, "Was Garibaldi here in Mexico, Pedro?"

"*Si*, Stuart, few people realize the Italian revolutionary spent time in Latin America fighting here too for the cause of independence. In fact, he married a woman from Uruguay. In the struggle for independence from Spain, many Latino revolutionaries were Freemasons. Ironically during the infamous Mexican-American War several of the American invaders, including their leader, General Zachary Taylor, were Freemasons as well."

Historian Juan Carlos was stunned by an aspect of the history of his country of which he had no knowledge. While aware of centuries of church hostility toward any questioning of its authority or Enlightenment notions of the separation of church and state, he had no idea of the influence of Freemasonry, which seemed to have flourished in Latin America for centuries. Now as he gazed with wonder at the panoply of Mexican history displayed on the walls of the Lautaro Lodge, he realized there was so much more to learn about his own country. Again, he was reminded how important it was to bear in mind throughout Latin America, Roman Catholicism had been imposed on deeply spiritual indigenous populations who revered the forces of nature.

Drummond was dazzled by the realization his beloved fraternity had managed to flourish and pursue its ideals of reason and service to God in Latin America.

"So much to learn and so much to share with Elizabeth and Dame Frances...how little we know about the so-called New World!" he confessed to Juan Carlos. "That so many revolutionaries were Freemasons could not have pleased Church authorities—to say nothing of the Women's Ordination Conference today! I can't help but wonder whether the same issues are playing out before our eyes in the Convent...."

As Guzman introduced Drummond, who shared a traditional handshake with each of the two dozen or so Mexican compatriots assembled in a circle, he was overwhelmed by a sense of Universal Brotherhood and felt immediately at home. As in London, a closed Bible was placed on the altar in the center of the chamber along with a Square and Compass and three tall, lighted candles representing North, South, and the Temple. Even though the ceremony was conducted in Spanish, Drummond followed every aspect of the ritual.

A hush settled over the chamber as the Brothers entered carrying Masonic and Mexican flags. In the silence Drummond marveled at the chain of events that had brought him here: a death at the Warburg Institute, his fortuitous introduction to Frances Yates and Giordano Bruno, and, above all, a vibrant, dynamic wife with whom he was deeply in love and for whom he was profoundly grateful. Now, half a world away in Mexico, he was humbled by a heightened awareness of the universality of the traditions of Freemasonry, the Hermetic worldview, and Tarot.

The sense of brotherhood, spirituality, and dignity in the ceremonial temple room thoroughly appealed to Juan Carlos. Ritual sanctity, which had become meaningless for him in the church, prevailed at the Lodge. Here it lacked the rigid autocracy of Roman Catholicism, and infused with elements of the Hermetic tradition, he realized how much he missed it.

After the ceremony, there was an excellent dinner in the stately dining room of perfectly cooked beef with fiery, fresh salsa, accompanied by a robust Miguel red wine, followed by layers of lemon cake and snifters of hearty Presidente brandy and hefty Camacho cigars. The Brothers, who seemed at ease with English, peppered Drummond, seated at the right of el Maestro de Adoracion, with questions about London Grand Lodge, its rituals, and centuries of history and tradition.

Later when he returned to the Majestic, Elizabeth, who had waited up for him, was nestled in bed with her new book of Mexican poetry. Quickly joining her, Drummond shared the evening's revelations, then listened attentively as she recounted details of her provocative dinner with Frances.

As they nestled in each other's arms, Elizabeth surmised, "Doesn't it seem, Stuart, as if all spiritual roads seem to intersect in Mexico?"

Chapter Fifty-Seven

At eight o'clock Saturday morning, Juan Carlos was waiting in the lobby for Frances. An hour earlier she was awakened with a phone call from the front desk and a fortifying breakfast tray of hot tea, sugary churros, and chunks of fresh, sweet pineapple delivered to her room.

After a short drive to a small local airport not far outside the city, they were escorted onto a small plane seating only a dozen or so passengers, mostly tourists staying at other hotels in the city. When they had fastened their seatbelts in the narrow, hard seats and taken off toward the Yucatan, a gracious male attendant, wearing a colorfully embroidered white cotton shirt, served the passengers hot coffee, tea, and cold drinks along with packages of crunchy *bizcochitos*. Soon they were soaring over a lush, green jungle. Within an hour, Frances was astounded with her first glimpse of the fabled ancient city of Chichen Itza. Although she had never visited Egypt, she hardly expected to see a colossal pyramid in Mexico of all places.

"The scale of this architectural feat is stunning, and that it so closely resembles the pictures of those in Egypt makes anyone wonder if the similarity is mere coincidence," Frances conjectured.

Chichen Itza

Most of the tourists appeared to be American, and everyone listened attentively as the English-speaking guide explained the pyramid had been constructed by the Toltecs a thousand years ago. Situated on a sacred well, it was positioned to precisely record the solstices and equinoxes. At the spring equinox, the reflection of the sun on the massive sculpture of a giant serpent's head at the base of the North side was a sign to the Toltecs to begin spring planting.

"How did they know?" Frances marveled.

The guide explained through a narrow slit carved into the stone roof of the observatory, named el Caracol (snail) because of the narrow spiral staircase inside, the Toltecs could track equinoxes, solstices, eclipses and Venus's 584-day cycle and trajectory across the heavens.

"Astounding!" Frances exclaimed. "Truly, Juan Carlos, I am overwhelmed and grateful to you for bringing me to this remarkable site."

"Dama Francesca, I have a further proposal. Since it is an extraordinary experience, I wonder if you would consider ascending to the top of the pyramid with me."

Fervently Juan Carlos yearned his mentor experience ascending the massive ancient structure, which for him and many Mexicans was a holy site where he had experienced spiritual transcendence and was certain—especially in the context of the Hermetic tradition—Dame Frances would as well.

"My dear, how is that possible?" Frances scoffed. "Never in another thousand years could I manage to climb those giant stones."

But it seemed there were ways to transport even an aging and far from lithe matron to the apex of Chichen Itza...

While Juan Carlos entered into negotiations with the numerous official guides milling about the pyramid, Frances strolled along the base, examining the hieroglyphs carved into the ancient stone. Serpents were everywhere.

The serpent is omnipresent but here appears to be a sign of renewal rather than evil and temptation as depicted in the Judeo-Christian tradition, Frances reflected. *How did we twist it all around in Europe? Wasn't this sin-laden worldview, promulgated by the Church, what Bruno was trying to transform with his message of universality?*

Was it her perpetually over-active imagination or her recent article for *The New York Review of Books,* which lingered in her mind, here too she was reminded of Tarot? Or could an ancient pyramid in the midst of the Mexican jungle be confirmation of her theory the illustrations on the cards were universal symbols?

Later when incredibly she found herself at the flat apex of the ancient pyramid, she couldn't help but think of the Tarot Magician's table. Since exploring the Tarot, Frances was convinced Catholic and Anglican priests replicated the Magician's ancient ritual as they celebrated the Eucharist. Perhaps the Mayans used the apex of the pyramid to perform the very same ritual of transformation.

In any event, one recurring image reminded her of the Fool, who launches his spiritual journey at the beginning of every deck of the Major Arcana. Along with the serpents, was it another mere, albeit extraordinary, coincidence two intertwined triangles appeared to replicate exactly the Masonic square and compass? Frances couldn't wait to share the image with Freemason Inspector Drummond.

The sacred pyramid never failed to transport Juan Carlos. Fervently he yearned to share its sense of timelessness and universality with Dame Frances. Remarkably he had arranged for a way to transport the aging, corpulent scholar to be transported to the top of the ancient structure.

Marjorie G. Jones

"*No es problema, Señor,*" one of the sturdy, indigenous guides stationed at the base of the pyramid had informed Juan Carlos with a shrug and a smile, glancing at Frances, as he displayed a large, sturdy canvas sling. "If *la señora* wishes, two of us can easily carry her all the way to the top. We have managed much heavier pilgrims!"

"Dama Francesca?" Juan Carlos apprehensively questioned his mentor as he proposed the daring expedition.

Valiantly and without giving it a second thought, esteemed Dame Frances Yates exclaimed, "Onward!" and soon found herself strapped onto a sling suspended on the strong shoulders of two indigenous Americans, as they made their arduous way up giant blocks of stone to the apex of an ancient looming pyramid.

As much as she tried to maintain her dignity—or at least thought she did—for the first time in her long life Frances Yates wished she owned a pair of trousers. Her straw chapeau notwithstanding, beads of sweat rolled down her forehead, and her armpits felt as if they were covered with glue. Certainly, skirts were not made for climbing pyramids, as helplessly she watched hers crawl closer to the tops of her garters. Recalling the fantastic exploits of Gertrude Bell and the Sisters of Sinai, who discovered the Hidden Gospels in the Middle East, she marveled, *How on earth did they cope with camels in long skirts and corsets?*

With Juan Carlos hovering on one side and an English-speaking guide on the other, Frances learned each plane of the four-sided pyramid, known as El Castillo, had 91 steps that together with the apex equaled the 365 days in a year on the Mayan calendar. Another coincidence?

When they were certain she was safe, secure, and steady on the broad stone platform at the apex, Juan Carlos gave Frances water from a canteen and moved a few steps away to allow her an unobstructed view of the vista. Leaning back against the slanted apex of the ancient stone pyramid, in pellucid silence that nearly took her breath away, Dame Frances Yates was transported beyond time and place.

Occasionally she experienced a somewhat similar sensation during communion at Claygate, but the experience at the top of an ancient sacred pyramid overwhelmed her. With a sense of timeliness, universality, and proximity to the Divine, Frances was transported beyond time and place. Awash in wonder, she thanked the Great Mother for new friends and contemplated the seemingly random (Were they really?) chain of events that had led her a half-world away from London to the Mexican jungle. Then she considered Bruno and Juana, two martyrs spiritually linked over time and place.

Gazing toward the East, she murmured softly, "Mexico *is* syncretism."

As long as she lived, the spiritual transcendence Frances Yates experienced atop an ancient pyramid in Mexico would remain among her most cherished memories.

Chapter Fifty-Eight

In the meantime, that same morning when Inspector Guzman arrived at the Convent, Drummond and Elizabeth were waiting in the entry.

Wasting no time on formalities, Guzman greeted them, "Good morning, *mis amigos*, if you would, please proceed to the library. In a few minutes I will join you there, but first I must visit the office of the Abadesa."_

When Guzman climbed the narrow stone stairway leading to the Chancery and entered, he found the Abadesa and Sor Gertrudis at their desks; both rose from their seats immediately.

Noting his grim demeanor, the Abadesa greeted him hesitantly, "*Buena dia*, Inspector."

Wasting no time on niceties, Guzman directed, "Abadesa, will you please summon Sor Carmela to the library and then join us there?"

For strategic and psychological reasons Guzman had decided to move the interrogations and any possible confrontations to the library where the crime had occurred. The Abadesa nodded curtly and instructed Gertrudis to summon Carmela._

A few minutes later, looking pale and drawn, Carmela joined them in the library. The nun seemed to grimace when Guzman indicated with an open hand the empty chair at the one side of the long table, where he and Abasdesa sat at either end with Drummond and Elizabeth on the other side.

Abruptly Guzman opened the interview, "Sor Carmela, I regret to inform you last evening Father Manuela Gonzales was arrested at the Cardinal's residence and charged with the murder of Sor Angela. Currently he is incarcerated and awaiting an appearance before the city magistrate."

Clutching the narrow, hard arms of the wooden chair, Carmela gasped. Bowing her head, the Abadesa murmured, "*Dia mia....*"

Beneath the table Elizabeth and Drummond clasped hands.

"Among others, Father Manuel's fingerprints, as are those of all *religiosos* in Mexico City, are on file with the diocese and have been detected on the encyclopedia. Since your fingerprints also were detected on the encyclopedia, once again I must ask, Sor Carmela, were you also in the library last evening?"

"I was not! Of course, my fingerprints are on the book," Carmela hissed. "Like most other books in the library, I have touched the encyclopedia several times! What about those of that horrible old English woman? Since she removed the encyclopedia from Sor Angela's arms, weren't hers found as well?"

"Admittedly some unknown fingerprints also were detected, but I am certain, if required, Dama Francesca Yates would submit her fingerprints."

"She will," Elizabeth confirmed.

"But we also know, Sor Carmela, that Dama Francesca was not in the Convent last evening, while you *were*. What's more, we know you had the opportunity to enter the Abadesa's office late yesterday afternoon while the Eucharist, which you did not attend, was being celebrated in the chapel. Since the office was unlocked and no one else there at the time, you easily you could have removed the key to the desk where the encyclopedia was kept."

"You have no proof, Inspector," Sor Carmela countered boldly.

"But unfortunately, Sor Carmela, we *do* have Father Manuel's confession of your plan to leave the library desk unlocked for him. Furthermore, Sores Maria and Lucia have confirmed his presence in the convent Wednesday evening. When they had finished their chores in the kitchen and were returning to their cell, Sor Maria and Sor Lucia reported seeing someone resembling Father Garcia walking up the stairs to the library."

Carmela gasped and slumped in her chair, then screeching, pointed her finger at her superior, "This is all your fault, Teresa! With your absurd feminist notions of a Great Mother and daring to conduct the Eucharist yourself...you are a heretic and are unqualified to lead this convent!"

Though she spoke only sporadic Spanish, Elizabeth had no difficulty absorbing the tenor of the diatribe—especially the key word *heretica*. Even

Drummond, witness to many similar confrontations, followed the gist of what Carmela was saying.

"Like our heroine Sor Juana!" the Abadesa retorted firmly without a moment's hesitation. Addressing her adversary directly and calmly, she vowed, "As long as I have breath in my body, her legacy will be honored and sustained in the Convent of San Jeronimo."

Then turning to Elizabeth, Drummond, and Guzman, she said in flawless English, "Isn't it tragic four centuries after the martyrdoms of Sor Juana de la Cruz and Giordano Bruno, the Inquisition continues to thrive in Mexico!"

Chapter Fifty-Nine

Perils notwithstanding, Frances remained enthralled as she made the precarious trip down the steep stone steps of the ancient pyramid. Gazing downward wasn't nearly as intriguing as the journey toward the apex; in fact, it was downright terrifying. By the time Frances and Juan Carlos returned to Mexico City it was 7:00 P.M. It had been an extraordinary and unforgettable day. With enormous relief and Juan Carlos at her elbow, Frances entered the lobby of the Majestic. Overwhelmed with revelation and exhaustion, rather than another festive dinner, Frances wanted nothing more than a hot tub, the business of smoking, and dinner on a tray in her room. More than anything she needed quiet time alone to process the stunning revelations of her journey to the ancient pyramid.

But when they entered the lobby, Frances and Juan Carlos were startled to encounter Elizabeth and Drummond waiting for them in the club chairs near the front desk. With foreboding somber faces, both rose to greet the two travelers.

"What is it?" Frances asked at once. "Please don't tell me there has been another death in the convent."

Elizabeth's hand patted her arm, while Drummond reassured her, "There has not, Dame Frances. Instead there has been quick resolution of the sordid events."

"Tell me, please," Frances sighed with relief, as she sank into one of the commodious chairs, and the others followed her example.

Out of nowhere, as if magically summoned, Jésus appeared at the table. "Perhaps, Jésus, you can bring us some hot tea," Elizabeth urged and then began to relate the afternoon's startling denouement. "Dame Frances, once again your theory regarding the sequence of events was right on target. As you suspected and we learned today, it was not Sor Angela who attempted to remove the book from the library. Instead she was attempting to protect it from someone else who was caught with proverbial red hands doing just that."

"Was it Sor Carmela?" Frances asked, as at last she idled her Deliciado and sipped some hot tea Jésus efficiently delivered to the low, glass-topped coffee tables before the chairs.

"Yes and no," Drummond nodded equivocally with a raised eyebrow. "While the list of suspects was not extensive, Inspector Guzman, Elizabeth and I were focused on Father Manuel's overt hostility toward the book and community. Still we felt it imperative to investigate whether other nuns had been complicit. Including, by the way, the Abadesa, since it occurred to us she may have wanted to remove the book from the library to protect it from damage or disappearance.

"Point well taken, Inspector," Frances nodded. "Frankly I hadn't thought of that possibility."

Drummond continued, "Nonetheless it was no surprise under questioning Sor Carmela erupted and confessed she had taken the key earlier in the day while you and the others were participating in the Eucharist. Then she left the desk drawer open for Father Manuel.

"Poor Angela, who was looking for something to read that night, arrived in the library just as Father Manuel was removing the book from the desk. When she attempted to stop him, they struggled, and he shoved her. Clutching the encyclopedia, Angela fell, hitting her head on the edge of the desk."

"Just as you surmised, Dame Frances," Elizabeth reaffirmed.

Exhaling slowly, Frances sat back and staring into space, observed thoughtfully, "Last year the Warburg and now here in the convent of revered Sor Juana: How remarkable and tragic such passions and politics can fester and be unleashed in sacred spaces! Then again, like Bruno, although perhaps not as brutally, Juana too was subjected to the wrath of the Inquisition. Perhaps, as they say, history does repeat itself, although to me that has always seemed a simplistic notion to explain similarly convoluted situations."

"That the Church's orthodoxy and ferocity persist in our own time is equally disturbing to me, Dame Frances," Elizabeth added. "Although, as you know, I am not a Roman Catholic, it seems, following the example of the Anglicans, the notion of a Universal Church would only be enhanced with the introduction of women and married priests. Centuries later the issue seems to center around perceived threats to traditional male power."

"Yet, ironically, as I have learned this week in Mexico," Frances acceded, "the Mexican church is uniquely steeped in matriarchal reverence for the Virgen de Guadalupe or Great Mother. In this cultural context an observer could surmise that the presence of women priests would be especially appealing."

"What do you think about all of this, Juan Carlos?" Elizabeth turned toward her young colleague and host.

"First and foremost, Elizabeta and Dama Francesca, I terribly regret this ugliness has occurred during your visit. To say the least, I had intended other activities. Yet I must observe notwithstanding the extraordinary reverence for la Virgen in Mexico, the institutional church throughout Latin America maintains a firm grip on the local hierarchy. To say this implies men only is an understatement. Of course, this is also an issue of class that dates back centuries and is rooted in a European sense of superiority over indigenous cultures. To this day, whether one is a *criollo* of pure Spanish lineage or *mestizo* of mixed heritage, as most Mexicans are, is noteworthy."

"Class, of course," Frances affirmed. "How often we old-fashioned historians overlook its influence and implications! But tell us, Inspector, what will happen to Sor Carmela?"

Drummond, who per usual had sat quietly, sipping tea while observing and absorbing the conversation, placed his cup on the saucer. "According to Inspector Guzman, who took her into custody this morning, out of respect for her age and years of service, rather than the city jail she will be held in custody at the city hospital until Monday morning when she will be arraigned. Apparently, the Cardinal has provided an attorney for the diocese to represent her. Since it appears the death was more or less accidental, she may be able to avoid spending time in prison and instead be sent to do penance in extreme seclusion for the rest of her life."

All conferees concurred this seemed appropriate punishment, and when Juan Carlos conveyed Abadesa Teresa's invitation they reunite at ten on Sunday for a church service in the convent, they readily agreed.

Chapter Sixty

After an hour or so of debriefing, Elizabeth made an announcement, "My friends, I have a confession."

Her three colleagues turned anxiously toward her, as she declared, "I am starving!"

Magically all of the guacamole had been consumed. Exchanging smiles, Frances's accomplices noted the dab of green goo at the edge of her bottom lip. By now it was eight o'clock and clearly to each of her colleagues Frances was exhausted. Her exhilarating expedition to the top of an ancient pyramid in the Mexican jungle, the unraveling of the death in the convent, and a week of sightseeing in blistering heat had rendered her virtually numb, so when Juan Carlos suggested a light supper at a nearby bistro, she declined, saying she preferred dining alone quietly in her room. What she needed most was a cool tub and time for reflection.

"Of course, Dame Frances," Elizabeth understood immediately. "On the way to your room let's stop by the dining room and ask Jésus to send a tray to your room whenever you wish."

"Thank you, my dear—that would be lovely!" Frances responded gratefully, as all four rose from their chairs. With Elizabeth at her elbow, Frances tottered across the lobby.

Following Frances's lead, Juan Carlos admitted he too was depleted by the day's excursion. Relieved not to be called upon to host another festive dinner, he excused himself, informing his guests he would join them for church in the convent in the morning. Then on Monday morning he would pick them up at nine for the drive to the airport.

Equally drained by their intense and emotional day, Elizabeth and Drummond also decided to stay at the Majestic for dinner. Sensing their fatigue and somber mood, Jésus brought a steaming tureen of chicken soup with rice, chunks of chicken, and fresh spinach and warm quesadillas, followed by a comforting caramel custard smothered by a melee of fresh tart berries.

Chapter Sixty-One

As she leaned back and soaked in the hot, soapy tub where she always did some of her best thinking, Frances exhaled a satisfying Deliciado and reflected on—beyond resolving another murder—what she had learned during her extraordinary week in Mexico.

To begin, and most remarkably, the Hermetic tradition had been transmitted to Mexico, or perhaps—and here was an epiphany—it had been here all along, embedded in the indigenous worldview.

Then there was syncretism and the ease with which the persona of the Virgin Mother with the Corn Goddess Tonantzin had melded into a unique and revered female deity.

Suddenly an extraordinary thought occurred to Frances. Sitting bolt upright in the tub, she exclaimed aloud, "What if the Hermetic tradition originated here in Latin America and was transmitted from here to Europe by explorers and missionary priests rather than the other way around? After all, Spaniards and Portuguese were here at least a full century before Bruno began his peregrinations through Europe. How arrogant and ethnocentric we Europeans are!"

As has occurred throughout her long career when she wrestled with new concepts, the seasoned scholar's still vibrant creative mind unfurled. "While the Great Mother is omnipresent and revered here in Mexico, in Europe she has been more or less overshadowed for centuries by patriarchal oppression and the political forces that brought death and destruction to Bruno.

"How is it possible the forces of the Inquisition seem to be alive and thriving and perhaps, four centuries later, the cause of another tragic martyrdom here in Mexico? No wonder Walker's encyclopedia is anathema to them—poor dear Sor Angela!"

By now her cigarette was a stub, the water had grown tepid, and Frances realized how hungry and tired she was. Clutching a handrail on the side of the tub, she heaved herself up and over the side onto the plush blue bathmat and into the fresh, white terrycloth robe hanging on the back of the door. A half-hour later, still wrapped in her thick robe, Frances heard a gentle knock at her door. When she opened it, she was delighted to see smiling Jésus with a cart on which sat a small china cup of purple and white violets and several silver-plated platter covers.

"How lovely! Bless you, Jésus! What have you brought?"

"Since you are leaving Mexico *manana*, Dama Francesca, I thought you should have a special supper. We say in Mexico, '*Esta casa es su casa.*'"

For her last meal in Mexico, Jésus had prepared a lovely tray composed of cold yogurt soup with bits of fresh fruit, baked chicken, warm tortillas with (of course) a bowl of guacamole, and caramel custard with chocolate cookies for dessert. Along with two crystal goblets, a cold bottle of mineral water, and a small carafe of *jerez* complemented the feast.

With doors overlooking the Zócalo ajar she could hear lilting guitars. As she gazed at Rivera's *alcatraces* Frances continued to attempt to corral and sort through her rampant thoughts. Among them was the realization, along with a significant banknote, she must leave a note of thanks on her tray for her charming steward Jésus.

Chapter Sixty-Two

At ten on Sunday morning, Juan Carlos met his colleagues in the lobby of the Majestic, where they had shared a simple breakfast. Once again, he escorted them across the Zócalo, which was much quieter and more subdued than on a weekday. For this morning's service, Frances wore her new chapeau along with a white, ruffled blouse under her dark blazer and ankle-length skirt. On her lapel a small corsage of fragrant orange blossoms Juan Carlos presented to her when he called for them.

"How remarkably thoughtful," Frances murmured as the young Mexican scholar she had grown to love like a son pinned the delicate flowers to her jacket.

Instead of her usual baseball cap, Elizabeth, dressed in dark slacks with a light blue cotton blazer, wore a new chapeau. A perfect souvenir, it was a gift from her husband from a boutique near the Zócalo. Soft red straw with two bright pink flowers stitched one over the other under the right side of the wide brim, it both shaded her eyes and flattered her mature, softly lined and now slightly bronzed fair complexion. As always, Drummond wore his uniform of navy blazer, fresh white shirt, and striped tie. For a change of pace on their last morning in Mexico, Drummond switched from his usual Witch Hazel and dared the aroma of citrus Calacas after-shave Elizabeth purchased for him in an apothecary near the Majestic.

"Why, Stuart, you could be mistaken for a Latino!" she teased as she nestled at his neck and stroked the smooth, strong cheeks she cherished.

At the entry to the convent they were greeted by Sor Susana, who greeted and escorted them to the darkened chapel, lit only by thick, handmade, beeswax lily-scented candles. There the Abadesa and other *monjas* were singly softly.

The Abadesa greeted them and softly taking each of their hands said, "*Buenos dias, mis queridos amigos.*"

As light filtered through the centuries-old stained glass windows, the stark, arched chapel was in effect an invitation to step back in time to the 1600s. Two tall, slender vases of vibrant yellow *alcatraces* complimented the large, plain, golden cross over the altar, covered with antique brocade, embroidered with gold thread and lush pomegranates.

When they created them, Elizabeth wondered, as she brushed her fingers lightly across the thick threads, *did the* religiosas *know—or, if they've studied the* Woman's Encyclopedia, *do they realize today—the red juice and plentiful seeds of the pomegranate symbolize Mother Earth and fertility?*

Several rows of simple wooden chairs were set in a semi-circle facing the table before the altar. When the guests and *religiosas* were seated, the Abadesa invited the group to join hands, and after a moment of silence the service began. In the corner, Sor Gertrudis played a melodic verse on the piano. How they mourned the sweet voice of martyred Sor Angela! Then the Abadesa rose from her chair, and in English began to speak directly to her guests, as Sor Susana translated softly for the other *monjas.*

"Cherished Friends, while our hearts are broken by the terrible events you have witnessed in the Convent, at the same time we also are grateful for your presence among us. Without it, it is unlikely the mystery could be resolved so quickly. Indeed I believe with all my heart the Great Mother sent you here and now to guide us through this trial. Further, as tragedy frequently and ironically affords opportunity, I fervently pray this one will lead us to refocus our prayers and energies on those ideals of spiritual and intellectual enlightenment and renewal established three centuries ago by our blessed Sor Juana. Now in her sacred spirit I invite each of you to share this ancient and sacred meal of bread and wine...."

As the Abadesa gestured toward the altar, Elizabeth reached for Frances's wrinkled hand. Quite unexpectedly, large, warm tears had begun to spill down her cheeks. Frances, too, wiped the network of wrinkles around her eyes with a frayed lace hanky that had belonged to her mother. Even seasoned Drummond found he had to swallow a lump in his throat.

Although she had witnessed the week's earlier service, once again Frances was moved as, bowing over the elements, the Abadesa declared this morning's Mass would be celebrated in honor the memory of dear departed Sor Angela. Although the Abadesa conducted the ritual in Spanish, Frances followed every word.

"The Lord be always with you."

"And with thy spirit."

"Life up your hearts."

"We lift them to the Lord."

"Let us give thanks to the Lord our God."

"It is meet and right to give thanks and praise."

Then facing the Holy Table, the Abadesa continued, "It is very meet, right, and our bounden duty, that we should at all times and in all places give thanks unto thee, O Lord, holy Mother, almighty, everlasting God."

Clearly each of the Anglophones heard and comprehended her emphasis of the word "Madre" rather than "Padre."

How bold! Frances reflected.

For Elizabeth, a Unitarian, it was a unique experience. Lately she had attended occasional Anglican services with Drummond, who never failed to comment regarding similarities between the Anglican Mass and Masonic traditions.

Chagrined, he admitted to himself it was disquieting to witness the ceremony being presided over by a woman. *No wonder Father Manuel was enraged!*

"Doctora Elizabeta, will you please read the lesson for us? It is from the *Gospel of Mary*."

Elizabeth, who had read Elaine Pagels's *Gnostic Gospels*, was enormously flattered by the invitation to participate. The *Gospel* was from the *Nag Hammadi Bible*, an ancient collection of early Christian Coptic texts discovered in Egypt in the 1940s. Of course, the Convent library would have a copy.

In an English translation, the passage regarding the appearance of the resurrected Christ to Mary Magdalene had been chosen by the Abadesa and highlighted in faint red pencil:

"Peter questioned them about the Savior: 'Did he really speak with a woman without our knowledge and not openly? Are we to turn about and all listen to her? Did he prefer her to us?'

Then Mary wept and said to Peter, 'My brother Peter, what do you think? Do you think that I thought this up myself in my heart, or that I am lying about the Savior?' Levi answered and said to Peter, If the Savior made her worthy, who are you indeed to reject her? Surely the Savor knows her very well. That is why he loved her more than us.'"

Later Elizabeth remarked to Frances and Drummond, given the startling text, it was a wonder, along with the *Woman's Encyclopedia*, Father Manuel didn't attempt to remove the *Nag Hammadi Gospels* as well from the Convent!

The Elements consisted of paper-thin, triangular corn meal wafers, prepared by Sores Maria and Lucia according to a centuries-old recipe recorded in the Convent cookbook. When he visited the Convent each week, Father Manuel consecrated the wafers. The pale, sweet wine came from the vineyard of another convent in the Yucatan.

Again, unexpectedly, the Abadesa invited Frances and Elizabeth to bring the Elements, waiting in an ornate silver goblet and heavy bowl on a table at the side of the chapel to the altar. The significant weight of the vessels was impressive.

Like carrying history itself, Frances thought.

Both Frances and Elizabeth were honored to be asked to participate in the ancient universal ritual, and when they returned to their chairs, instinctively they again clasped hands.

More or less a spiritual maverick, Juan Carlos sat humbly at Frances's left and with wonder witnessed the apparent spiritual elation of his American and British friends unfold before his eyes. That it should be taking place in the historic Convent of his beloved Sor Juana compounded his awe and pleasure.

For Frances the symbolic transformation of the bread and wine into the body and blood of Christ was a symbol of the potential spiritual transformation of everyone's life. It was a ritual she cherished but certainly never expected to experience in an ancient convent in Mexico! Kneeling on a thick brocade cushion, Frances cupped her hands and received the thin wafer from the Abadesa, followed by a sip of wine from the silver cup administered by Sor Susana.

"The Gifts of God for the People of God...."

As the crisp corn wafer melded into the sweet wine in her mouth and visions of her extraordinary week wafted through her brain, Frances was transported.

With another break from Catholic tradition, all attendees, regardless of creed, were invited by the Abadesa to participate in the ritual. Remarkably, therefore, the ceremony was also a transcendent experience for Elizabeth, who had never received communion. Kneeling next to Drummond, their elbows touching, the concept of the transformation of two elements into a new substance enhanced her gratitude and sense of closeness to her new husband. As they returned to their seats, the bread and wine lingering in their mouths, she reached for his strong hand, which clasped hers firmly.

From *Hero with a Thousand Faces to* the Warburg Institute to Dame Frances Yates, *Bruno and the Hermetic Tradition* to Tarot, the *Woman's Encyclopedia*, the Divine Spouse, Sor Juana de la Cruz, and the Virgen de Guadalupe—the links in the chain that had brought them to a convent in Mexico overwhelmed Elizabeth. When she began to softly cry, Drummond stroked her hand while the Abadesa pronounced the closing words of the service:

"The peace of God which passeth all understanding, keep your hearts and minds in the knowledge and love of God, and of his Son Jesus Christ our Lord, and the blessing of God Almighty, the Mother/Father, Son and Holy Ghost, be amongst you and remain with you always. Amen."

Chapter Sixty-Three

At the conclusion of the ritual and a final lyrical hymn, the Abadesa invited her guests to lunch in the refectory, where Maria and Lucia eagerly awaited and escorted them to their places. Two long tables had been set and covered with starched, time-worn white linen. Heavy, ornate, antique Mexican silver flatware lined each place. Jars of thick, hand-painted Mexican pottery brimming with fresh wildflowers arranged among white blossoms from the Convent garden were placed in the center.

Hand-painted name cards with wildflowers marked each place. On one side of the head table, Frances was seated at the right hand of the Abadesa with Elizabeth on her left. Both the aged English scholar and her American apprentice were pleased and flattered. Drummond and Juan Carlos were seated at either end of the table, while Juan Carlos and Sor Susana sat across from the Abadesa, Frances and Elizabeth. As she unfolded and placed the lovely, embroidered, white, starched napkin on her lap, Elizabeth exchanged smiles with Drummond while wondering whether the worn linen might also have touched the lips of Sor Juana.

At a second table with hands folded in their laps the other *religiosas* chatted quietly, occasionally nodding and exchanging soft smiles with their prestigious guests.

"Dama Francesca, will you please say grace?" the Abadesa requested, once again surprising her esteemed colleague. Although she dearly wished she had been given at least a few moments to prepare and collect her overflowing thoughts, Frances paused a few seconds, then bowed her head and in her gravely voice prayed aloud:

"Great Mother and Father, we give thanks from our deepest hearts for this remarkable and enlightening week in the Convent, new dear friends in beguiling Mexico, and especially the blessed legacy of brilliant Sor Juana de la Cruz. May she continue to guide and give us insight, and may each of us aspire and strive to follow her unique example of spiritual yearning enhanced by the life of the mind...Amen"

"Amen," they all said in unison, as the simple meal was served. First, shallow porcelain bowls of cool pineapple and strawberry soup with warm tortillas and platters of tender and mild Oaxaca cheese chunks with a relish of sweet pickled onions and carrots. For dessert Maria and Lucia prepared *capirotada*, a bread pudding, as the Abadesa explained, traditionally served during Holy Week, yet appropriate, she, Maria and Lucia determined, for this special occasion. Laden with cinnamon, vanilla, raisons, nuts, apple, and queso fresco, the rich concoction melted in Frances's mouth.

"Divine!" she proclaimed, as she scarped her bowl and eagerly accepted a generous second helping. Beyond her knowledge of Renaissance historiography, Frances Yates considered herself a *connoisseur* of bread pudding. The Mexican rendition was superb and immediately ascended to the top of her chart of culinary favorites!

Declining second helpings, Elizabeth and Drummond echoed her sentiments. "Probably under the circumstances," Elizabeth mused, "I should make an effort to refrain from licking my plate!"

Chapter Sixty-Four

The mood of the gathering was subdued but cordial. As they settled in and began to dine, the Abadesa turned to Frances, "Dama Francesca, an idea has occurred to me. When you return to England, I wonder if you might give thought to an imagined meeting or correspondence between Sor Juana and Giordano Bruno. After all, even though an ocean apart and separated by several decades, they shared a Hermetic worldview. Although Sor Juana wasn't burned by the Inquisition, she too suffered and was gravely punished by the same forces that resulted in her early death."

As if struck by lightning, Frances held her silver fork midair. "What a marvelous idea, Abadesa!"

As the concept of a meeting between the two extraordinary mystics took root in her still remarkably fertile brain, immediately she began to plot the outlines of an article.

Across the table she suggested to Juan Carlos, "Perhaps we three can correspond and, using original sources from the Convent's library, fashion an article for both English and Mexican publications."

"It would be an honor to collaborate with two such esteemed scholars," Juan Carlos exuded. "When shall we begin?" Then he added provocatively, "Should it be a scholarly endeavor or perhaps, Dama Francesca, for a change of pace we might attempt a bit of fiction."

"As you know, Juan Carlos I've never attempted fiction, but you may have come up with the appropriate context for such an imaginary encounter...Why not give it a try?" Pushing her chair away from the table, Frances turned to the Abadesa and *sotto voce* asked, "Abadesa, before leaving the Convent for the last time, do you think I might be permitted one more visit to Sor Juana's chambers? I would like very much to engrave her presence among my memories of Mexico."

"Come, *mia querida*," the Abadesa invited her at once, taking her hand and without further explanation to the other guests led Frances from the refectory.

Sensing an extraordinary moment and the need to linger in the refectory, Elizabeth, Drummond, and Juan Carlos mingled and chatted with the *religiosas*.

Chapter Sixty-Five

When they reached the hallowed chamber, the Abadesa informed Frances, "I will wait for you outside the door. For me it is always a powerful experience to be alone in the presence of Sor Juana."

As she entered the apartment for the second time—this time alone—Frances was awash with the sanctity of a holy place. That she should feel so in touch with a seventeenth-century Mexican nun astonished her. Then, she reminded herself, she also felt kinship with a sixteenth-century Italian priest. Of course, she understood it was their mutual spiritual universality articulated by the Hermetic tradition she admired and shared. Each mystic had been martyred for the same reasons. Now centuries later, here in Sor Juana's own sanctuary, another crime had been committed by the same forces.

How in this day and age could a message of reconciliation and reverence still be so threatening? Really it was frightening. Then...was it possible? Frances thought she heard Sor Juana's voice speaking directly to her—in English no less—urging her to stay strong, carry on with her work, and above all, the teaching of future generations of scholars and seekers. Momentarily she even imagined herself a *monja* like Juana or Teresa, worshipping and reading in a cloistered community. After all, in a way wasn't the Warburg, which had been a haven for nearly half a century, a similar environment?

Humbled by her revelation, Frances nodded to her portrait and uttered a quiet "*Gracias,* Sor Juana."

When Frances rejoined her in the corridor, comprehending what had transpired, Teresa took Frances's hand and together with bowed heads the two wise crones, one Mexican, one English, shared a prayer of thanks to the Great Mother for bringing them together in friendship and spiritual harmony.

Making the sign of the Cross on Frances's forehead, the Abadesa bid her farewell, "*Vaya con Dios, querida* Dama Francesca."

Chapter Sixty-Six

When the four colleagues left the convent and walked one last time toward the Zócalo, it was nearly two in the afternoon. While Frances remained spellbound by her encounter with Sor Juana, Elizabeth and Drummond were energized and eager to spend their last afternoon in Mexico City to full advantage. For Elizabeth, a visit to Casa Azul with Stuart was a priority.

"Please go ahead, my dears," Frances urged. "Truly I am quite satiated with new revelations, and in any event, believe it is time for siesta. Especially in light of the remarkable experience we have just shared in the Convent, nothing would please me more than another quiet evening at the Majestic with supper on a tray in my room and time to reflect and perhaps make a few notes in my journal."

Furthermore, as she whispered in an aside to Juan Carlos, it had occurred to Frances that Elizabeth and Drummond might appreciate at least one afternoon and evening to themselves in Mexico City.

"*Claro, Dama Francesca,*" Juan Carlos replied and informed his guests he must prepare for his classes the next day, but in the morning would call for them at nine for the drive to the airport.

Upon their return from Coyoacan and for their last dinner, their first by themselves in Mexico City, Elizabeth and Drummond decided to stroll through the dimly lit historic center to dine—per Juan Carlos's recommendation—at romantic and historic Cafe Tacuba.

"Perfect!" Elizabeth delighted, as they entered the vibrant bistro and were greeted by the sound of melodic guitars strummed by a small band of colorfully jacketed musicians on a small platform beyond the tables.

Certainly it was a further sign they were in the right place when they were escorted to a table facing a large reproduction of Cabrera's portrait of Sor Juana. Had unfailingly thoughtful Juan Carlos selected that very table while ordering the cold bottle of bubbly Mexican Cava resting in a bucket of ice alongside? Another reason he had recommended Tacuba, established in 1912, was Diego Rivera and his first wife and model Lupe Marin held their wedding banquet there. With dark wood, patterned tiles, elaborate stained glass windows in the highly arched ceiling, and shelves crammed with local art and memorabilia, Tacuba appeared more museum than restaurant.

Seated side by side with shoulders just touching, gazing at the riveting murals, they raised their glasses to one another.

"Alone at last, Stuart—to say the least it's been a unique honeymoon!" Elizabeth commented wryly, while reaching for his hand resting on the table.

"Indeed, my dear, if this week is an indication of future adventures, it appears it will be a stimulating journey," Drummond responded.

"As long as we're together, Stuart, I'll go anywhere with you," Elizabeth agreed.

"And I with you," the usually laconic Scotland Yard detective responded. Kissing her hand with a rare gesture of public affection, he presented her with a perfect magnolia blossom wrapped in green tissue, which he had purchased at the Zócalo while Elizabeth bathed before dinner.

"Juan Carlos informs me in Spanish, it is called *flor de Corazon*, flower of my heart. After so many years alone, having such a charming, intelligent, and valiant companion is a great and unexpected gift."

"And the hugs feel good too!" Elizabeth laughed, as tears spilled down her cheeks, "Really, Stuart, it's a skill at which you excel, and I feel enormously blessed. Thank you for your love and thoughtfulness!"

Bolstered by the compliment and the obvious effects of the Cava, Drummond's cheeks reddened as he turned to the menu and queried, "Now what delicacies shall we indulge ourselves for our last dinner in Mexico?"

To their added delight the newlyweds quickly discovered Tacuba cuisine complemented the ambiance.

Although aware to lose the pounds accumulated on enticing and mouth-watering Mexican food she would have to fast for weeks upon their return to London, which, baked beans notwithstanding, was considerably easier there, Elizabeth was compelled to order *atun Sor Juana* with fiery red salsa *con arroz*, while Drummond chose snapper sautéed in garlic butter. For dessert the newlyweds shared a towering lime-laced layer cake with a thin layer of sweet almond frosting, known as *Carlota de Limon* after the ill-fated empress, who resided briefly and tragically at Chapultepec.

Chapter Sixty-Seven

For her long trip home, Frances wore her new sombrero and carried a multi-colored, hand-woven straw basket crammed full of art books, travel brochures, and for reading on the plane, the novel Elizabeth had discovered at the English bookshop.

When they were called to board the plane to New York, with tears welling in her eyes and overflowing onto her wrinkled cheeks, Frances kissed those of her host. "How to thank you, dearest Juan Carlos? You and Mexico have enhanced my spiritual journey beyond my furthest imagination and wildest dreams. The past week has been an unforgettable adventure for which I shall be eternally grateful...*Muchas gracias, mi amigo*!"

Gathering the aged, rotund scholar into his strong arms, the tall, gallant young Mexican responded, "*Querida Dama Francesca*, nothing ever can adequately repay you for what you and Giordano Bruno have taught me, which in turn I will make every effort to impart to future generations of my students here in Mexico. May God and the spirits of Sor Juana and Giordano Bruno keep you safe and well for many years to come!"

As they embraced, Juan Carlos slipped a small, black velvet sack tied with a string into Frances's hand.

"A memento from Mexico," he said.

When she untied the sack Frances discovered a silver brooch of an alcatraces blossom inlaid with turquoise, coral, and jade.

"Oh, my dear, it is beautiful," she whispered as tears welled in her eyes. Pinning it to the lapel of her worn tweed jacket, she exclaimed, "Always I will cherish the brooch and whenever I wear it will think of you and magical Mexico with gratitude and love."

Witnessing the tender scene, as the chain of events that had led her and her new husband to Mexico along with the extraordinary drama of the past week flooded her mind, Elizabeth too was overcome. Embracing her fellow Warburgian, she thanked him profusely and shared she now intended to devote her studies and teaching to learning more about Latin American history.

"And for that reason, Stuart and I have decided to return to Mexico for further exploration next year!"

"*Maravilloso!*" Juan Carlos nearly shouted. "There is so much more I want to show you. Among other sites, we'll be sure to take the Inspector to Chichen Itza and also visit the Orozco murals at Guadalajara, which some say rival the Sistine Chapel!"

Then turning to Drummond, the two men shared a manly *abrazo* during which Drummond said quietly, "*Gracias, amigo*, when next we meet, I expect to be able to call you 'Brother.'"

Epilogue

Soon after the denouement of the death in the Covent became known at the Vatican, where recently a more enlightened Jesuit had been elected Pope, Cardinal Mendoza was relieved of his duties. Replaced by a younger cleric, who had studied at Jesuit Fordham University in New York, currently the new Cardinal served as president of the Pontifical University of Mexico City, founded in the 1500s. Soon it was determined and confirmed officially when the time came, Sor Susana would succeed Teresa as Abadesa. Further it was reaffirmed by Rome the legacy of Sor Juana de la Cruz be sustained and perpetuated for future generations of scholars and disciples.

In exchange for the Vatican's request for clemency for Sor Carmela, Guzman and the authorities agreed she be expelled immediately from San Jeronimo and confined for the rest of her life in an isolated community of *religiosas* high in the mountains of southern Mexico where her penitence was to teach the poorest of indigenous Mexican children to read.

Bibliography

Bedford, Sybille. *A Visit to Don Otavio: A Mexican Odyssey* (NY Review of Books, 1953)

Chowning, Margaret. *Rebellious Nuns* (Oxford University Press, 2005)

Desmond, Lawrence Gustave. *Yucatan Through Her Eyes: Alice Dixon LePlongeon, Writer & Expeditionary Photographer* (UNM Press, 2009)

Desmond, Lawrence Gustave and Phyllis Mauch Messenger. *A Dream of Maya: Augustus and Alice Le Plongeon in Nineteenth-Century Yucatan* (Duke University Press, 1988)

Clark, Emily, editor. *Voices from and Early American Convent* (LSU Press, 2007)

Del Paso, Fernando. *News from the Empire* (Dalkey Archives Press, 1987)

Doerr, Harriet. *Consider This, Se ora* (Harcourt Brace, 1993)

Enrigue, Alvaro. *Sudden Death* (Riverhead Books, 2013)

Frahm, Sara. *The Cross and the Compass: Freemasonry and Religious Tolerance in Mexico* (2014)

Gavin, Catherine. *The Cactus and the Crown* (Palibrio, 1962)

Gill, Anton. Art Lover: A Biography of Peggy Guggenheim (Harper Collins, 2002)

Inglis, Frances Erskine. *Life in Mexico* (Prescott, 1843)

Keyes, Frances Parkinson. *The Grace of Guadalupe* (Catholic Book Club, 1952)

Lavrin, Asuncion. *Brides of Christ: Convent Life in Colonial Mexico* (Stanford University Press, 2008)

McVicker, Mary F. *Adela Breton: A Victorian Artist Amid Mexico's Ruins* (UNM Press, 2005)

Merrim, Stephanie, editor. *Feminist Perspectives on Sor Juana Ines de la Cruz* (Wayne State University Press, 1999)

Oleszkiewicz-Peralba, Malgorzata. *The Black Madonna in Latin America and Europe* (UNM Press, 2007)

Pagels, Elaine. *The Gnostic Gospels* (Penguin Random House, 1979)

Paz, Octavio. *Sor Juana or The Traps of Faith* (Harvard University Press, 1988)

Peden, Margaret Sayers, translator. *Poems, Protest, and a Dream: Selected Writings of Sor Juana de la Cruz* (Penguin Random House, 1997)

Reed, Alma. *Passionate Pilgrim: The Extraordinary Life of Alma Reed* (Marlowe, 1993)

Ridley, Jasper. *The Freemasons* (Constable, 1999)

Walker, Barbara. The Woman's Encyclopedia of Myths and Secrets (Harper and Row, 1983)

West, Rebecca. *Survivors in Mexico* (Yale University Press, 2003)

Notes

F rances Yates never visited Mexico.
Although he paid tribute to Frances Yates, the brilliant biography of Sor Juana de la Cruz by Octavio Paz was published in 1988, eight years after the death of Frances Yates.

To date *Giordano Bruno and the Hermetic Tradition* has not been translated into Spanish.

Nuns are no longer cloistered in the Convent of San Jeronimo, which is now the *Universidad del Claustro de Sor Juana* (University of the Cloister of Sor Juana).

For convenience the two Cabrera portraits, Sor Juana and Divine Spouse, have been relocated to the Convent of San Jeronimo. In fact, the portrait of Sor Juana resides at Chapultepec and *El Divino Esposo* at the Los Angeles Museum of Art.

Although my husband and I once climbed and shared a transcendent experience atop the great pyramid at Chichen Itza, for safety reasons tourists no longer are permitted to undertake the arduous climb.

Acknowledgments

Longtime colleague and friend Dr. Maria Enrico, chair of the Modern Languages department at CUNY, patiently, meticulously, and expertly edited *In the Convent*, thereby demonstrating, in fact, authors and their editors can remain friends.

For the past two decades, I have been fortunate to teach in college programs at two maximum security prisons for men: Sing Sing in Ossining, NY for Mercy College, Dobbs Ferry, NY, and for Villanova at Graterford/Phoenix in PA, where students excel and have taught me so much more than any historical insights I have relayed to them. Their talents, resolve, and determination are remarkable. Frequently I have been asked whether prison students are better in NY or PA, and always my response is, "Yes!" At both institutions students are accomplished, diligent, and unfailingly appreciative of the opportunity to learn. To me they exemplify three R's: Repentance, Redemption, and Restoration. And talk about a good investment: When prisoners are educated, recidivism rates drop to less than 2%!

For the past forty years I have been blessed with the support and encouragement of my husband, Jonathan C. Jones, who, through the peregrinations of my convoluted career and the challenge of compiling four books, has served as research assistant, business manager, travel agent, proofreader, and tireless sounding board. Crowning his many talents is endless TLC *par excellence*. Among our many adventures was an unforgettable visit to the

Yucatan, where together we climbed and, like Frances Yates in this story, experienced transcendence atop the great pyramid at Chichen-Itza.

Once again valiant computer consultant Jay Hummel (MCT) has rescued me from the jungle of technological challenges, which overwhelm me.

Finally, thank you, Dorrance—especially gracious Senior Publishing Services Consultant Katy Antimarino and Shaina Ott. Your professionalism and cordiality are unsurpassed, and it is the fortunate author who is invited to collaborate with your century-long tradition of excellence.